Shakespeare Lied

ESSENTIAL ESSAYS 85

Canada

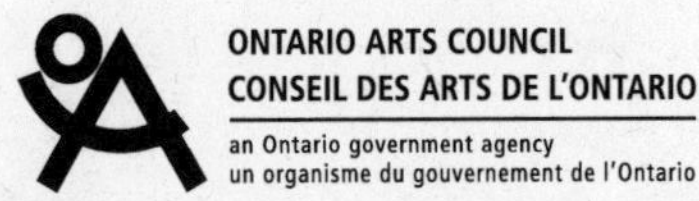

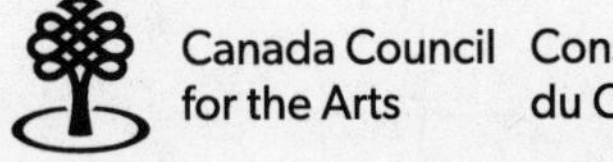

Conseil des arts
du Canada

Guernica Editions Inc. acknowledges the support of
the Canada Council for the Arts and the Ontario Arts Council.
The Ontario Arts Council is an agency of the Government of Ontario.

We acknowledge the financial support of the Government of Canada.

Sky Gilbert

Shakespeare Lied

GUERNICA EDITIONS

TORONTO • CHICAGO
BUFFALO • LANCASTER (U.K.)
2024

Guernica Founder: Antonio D'Alfonso

Michael Mirolla, editor
Interior and cover design: Rafael Chimicatti
Front Cover: Roman marble figure of Actaeon attacked by his hounds
2nd Century BC
Excavated from the Villa of Antoninus Pius

Guernica Editions Inc.
1241 Marble Rock Rd., Gananoque, ON K7G 2V4
2250 Military Road, Tonawanda, N.Y. 14150-6000 U.S.A.
www.guernicaeditions.com

Distributors:
Independent Publishers Group (IPG)
600 North Pulaski Road, Chicago IL 60624
University of Toronto Press Distribution (UTP)
5201 Dufferin Street, Toronto (ON), Canada M3H 5T8

First edition.
Printed in Canada.

Legal Deposit—Third Quarter
Library of Congress Catalog Card Number: 2023952541
Library and Archives Canada Cataloguing in Publication
Title: Shakespeare lied / Sky Gilbert.
Names: Gilbert, Sky, 1952- author.
Series: Essential essays series ; 85.
Description: Series statement: Essential essays ; 85
Identifiers: Canadiana (print) 20230620205 | Canadiana (ebook) 20230621929
ISBN 9781771839037 (softcover) | ISBN 9781771839044 (EPUB)
Subjects: LCSH: Shakespeare, William, 1564-1616—Criticism and
interpretation. | LCSH: Shakespeare, William, 1564-1616—Philosophy.
LCGFT: Literary criticism.
Classification: LCC PR2986 .G55 2024 | DDC 822.3/3—dc23

Contents

Prologue: Art

Modern art has rejected the mystical and the intuitive for the discursive and logical. Just go to any gallery these days and read the befuddling explanations that accompany the often ugly or boring creations. Conceptual art necessitates intellectual understanding — articulation that is quasi-scientific analysis. Serial composers like Arnold Schoenberg have made musical composition a function of mathematics. The 20th century has witnessed the much vaunted 'demise of the novel.' Of course people are still reading and writing popular fiction, but ex-novelist David Shields' book *Reality Hunger* (2010) celebrates his abandonment of narrative for writing that is more 'real.' Karl Ove Knausgaard's six-part opus *My Struggle* (he is considered by many to be the successor to both Joyce and Hemingway) is autobiographical fiction, describing ordinary daily occurrences in minute detail, using the real names of friends and family. Also significant is the recent rise of the neologism 'creative non-fiction': artists write creatively about actual people and events.

Today theatre collectives and directors produce works in which 'real people' (often non-actors, not playing 'characters') speak directly about their own social and political ideas, preaching noble notions about the environment, transphobia or anti-racism, in an endless array of one-person shows that resemble university lectures. Jordan Tannahill's recent book, *Theatre of the Unimpressed,* speaks approvingly of plays in which actors play themselves. Such plays have no plots, sets or costumes. Tannahill quotes theatre director Jacob Zimmer's contempt for traditional stage illusion: "'House to half. Stage to half. House out. Stage out. Shuffle shuffle shuffle. Lights up. I'm done! I'm done entirely!'" (29)[1] In contrast, this new avant-garde 'reality theatre' rarely tries to deceive us with artifice, and many modern theatre artists regard such attempts with contempt.

Universities now provide students practical information that will make them more employable, and more and more humanities courses are being cut. Since the 1930s, the humanities have felt the pressure to be more 'scientific.' In literature, this resulted in the 'New Criticism,' distancing literary theory from surmise, and excising speculation about the author's life and beliefs. The study of literature has given way to a literary science called semiotics. It's notable that Foucault (one of the most influential philosophers of the 20th century) began as a novelist, but eventually became a philosopher obsessed with the scientific analysis of language and words.

Our right brain is concerned with intuition and the 'big picture'; the left brain is obsessed with logic and detail. In *The Master and His Emissary*, Iain McGilchrist theorizes that we have left right brain function behind. We live in a scientific world dominated by the left brain. His theory is predicated on the notion that the left brain and the right were designed to work together, but the right brain — which was originally intended to be the master — has gradually ceded its power to the left (originally intended to be its emissary). For nearly four centuries western culture has rejected intuition, metaphor, and magic in favour of certainty, truth, and scientific knowledge. McGilchrist posits that, in the necessary partnership between the two sectors of the brain, the right side must always be the master. If it is not, we will come to relish "the substitution of information, and information gathering, for knowledge ... accompanied by a vast expansion of bureaucracy, systems of abstraction and control" (429).[2] Inevitably there will be increasing "focus on material things at the expense of the living. Social cohesion, and the bonds between person and person ... would be disconnected, perhaps actively disrupted." (431)[3]

The left brain cultural takeover began halfway through Shakespeare's life. Shakespeare wove fantastical narratives of magic, ghosts, and chivalric knights and their ladies during a general movement away from the sacred studies of grammar and rhetoric which had dominated the curriculum since the Middle Ages. Grammar (which does not have the same meaning in our modern use of the word) entailed studying life through poetry, not scientific observation. Poetry was considered truer than truth. Rhetoric theorized that language itself was noble, and that practical articulation of beautiful speech would make men better. But the beginning of the 17th century saw the popularization of the teachings of philosopher Petrus Ramus and the foundation of The Royal Society. In his *Dialecticae partitiones,* Ramus removed rhetoric from its pride of place in the academic curriculum. The Royal Society was instituted in 1660 to facilitate scientific experimentation and the logical propagation of knowledge. Shakespeare was at the centre of a culture war. His sympathies were with the medieval obsession with magic and mystery, over the rising philosophical tide of logic and fact.

Shakespeare's work often seems today to be written in another language, thus making it incomprehensible to many. But there is another aspect of Shakespeare's work that befuddles us. It is pure fiction, fantastical fantasy. For many young people — trained to nurture and respect their left brain function — this is a stumbling block. For though they may nurture a guilty passion for entertainment — in the form of super-hero movies, the fantasy world of video games, and Harry Potter — they expect more from art. Recently, when teaching *Hamlet* to a first year university class, I asked students: 'Is Hamlet mad?' The response was: 'It's not right to question whether or not Hamlet is mad. If people self-identify as having a mental illness, we must respect that and not challenge them.' As fiction itself becomes somewhat of an anachronism, students find it increasingly difficult to understand what it is.

What is valuable about Shakespeare is not only the essential beauty of his work, but his obsession with art, poetry, and representation. And though Shakespeare is certainly more than aware of the dangers of representation, the most eloquent argument he makes in favour of art is evident in the style of his work. Shakespeare lied. Shakespeare's plays and poems do not constitute a record of his time or cogent, useful historical analysis, and they certainly do not offer a prescription for a better life: They are significantly morally ambivalent. Thus, those who live in a world dominated by left brain activity might wonder — why bother? But Shakespeare's work is immensely valuable because the prevailing modern obsession with science would have us abjure lying. Picasso is reported to have said that 'art is a lie that makes us realize the truth.' But it would be more accurate to say that art creates another reality — one that is different than the world we know from day to day. Oscar Wilde said: 'Lying, the telling of beautiful untrue things, is the proper aim of Art' (55).[4] Art, in this way, is valuable to us — more valuable to us perhaps than life — because it is a '*thing-in-itself*' and, as such, it does not stand for something else.

* * *

In 1979 I founded a theatre — Buddies in Bad Times Theatre. I came bursting out of the closet, trumpets blaring, at age 29. Soon I was a small-time celebrity in Toronto after writing *Drag Queens on Trial*. A photo of me, dressed as Tarzan's Jane, was on the front page of the entertainment section of the *Toronto Star*. (I wore nothing but leopardskin rags, artfully placed.) I ran Buddies for seventeen years. After Buddies acquired a 350-seat theatre in downtown Toronto and grew into Canada's pre-eminent gay and lesbian theatre, I left.

Since then I have been writing and teaching. During Buddies' 40th anniversary season, I was delighted when artistic director Evalyn Parry announced a reading of my 1986 hit play *Drag Queens in Outer Space*. A week before the reading I wrote a controversial poem for my blog. I received an email from Evalyn Parry saying the 'community' was up in arms about my poem. I politely suggested Evalyn ignore the hysteria. In a return email she stated that, due to the offensive nature of my poem, the reading of my play would be cancelled. I was thus forced to remove myself from any association with the company that I founded many years ago.

The objection to my poem came from those who have very different notions about art than I do. Increasingly, people are not able to differentiate between rhetorical speech and daily conversation. My poem was treated as conversation and analyzed for its truthfulness. Yes, it was somewhat banal in style and not poetic in the traditional sense, so it might not appear to have been a poem; or, it might have been judged by some to be a bad poem. But the fact that my poem was unpoetic, or a lousy poem, is not why it outraged so many. They were engaged because they disagreed with what they perceived to be its message. But rhetoric can and must be differentiated from daily speech — or from scientific discovery — by the author's intentions. The purpose of art and rhetoric is only to be beautiful; poetry must be judged on its beauty alone.

Everyday speech is denotative language, utilizing words to express ideas, opinions, and information. Rhetoric, on the other hand, does not aspire to clarity. Rhetoric utilizes connotative language carefully crafted in a certain way in order to achieve a desired effect. In the best poetry, the style is the meaning. And rather than truth, we are presented with warring — yet engaging — visions.

Instead of judging the beauty of my poem, the critics treated it as a container for ideas. For them, the job of the audience is to tease out the specific meaning the author intended; the form is treated merely as a disguise. My poem certainly contained ideas. But whether those ideas were the intended meaning of the poem is another matter. When the playwright Bertolt Brecht was accused of being a communist on the witness stand of the House of Un-American Activities Committee in 1947, his plays were read aloud in court. But Brecht carefully differentiated his own opinions from the ideas expressed by characters in his plays. A writer employs a rhetorical technique (meaning a style, or a character voice) to persuade readers, and manipulate them into considering many sides of an issue. The artist — even when writing a poem — is assuming a fictional voice and hiding behind the rhetoric of the poem. The artist does not hide in order to be found. The artist hides in order to beguile you.

* * *

I must admit it. In the narrative about my controversial poem above, I conveniently omitted several facts I thought might offend you. Immediately after, deftly (I thought), I skipped to an analysis of the difference between rhetoric and speech to persuade you of my opinion.

These are the tricks of rhetoric and they have nothing at all to do with a fixed, immutable 'truth.'

It is significant that in all of this (even now), I have cultivated a humble tone through occasional self-deprecation. This is an ancient rhetorical technique, utilized extensively by Shakespeare. The rhetor, we quickly realize, whether the anonymous author of *The Sonnets*, or the various characters in Shakespeare's plays, is a deeply flawed human, who *at the very least* may, at certain times, take on a humble — even confused and bumblingly erratic tone — and, at most, may denigrate or even excoriate himself.

In the passage above, I purposefully omitted several significant facts. Though I mentioned I am a drag queen (a nod to the self-deprecation required of me as rhetor), I omitted some other things that might deeply offend you. Here goes. I have always identified myself publicly as a 'slut' and spoken proudly in praise of promiscuity, sex trade workers, and s/m sex. Also, in the1990s, I was allied with an AIDS radical group called HEAL, which challenged the notion that HIV causes AIDS. And finally (and perhaps most relevant in the context of this book), I am invested in another very 'radical' idea: that the 'real' Shakespeare was Edward de Vere, Earl of Oxford.

I am confessing all this in order to help you understand the complexity of any form of rhetorical manipulation. Or, perhaps, I am telling you this to further manipulate you — using Hermogenes' rhetorical technique of 'humility' (a technique, I repeat, that is consistently employed by Shakespeare) so that you will be fooled into thinking that what you are reading here is the truth.

What, after all, is one to believe?

This is the central question raised by Shakespeare's work, and it is no accident that it is also the foundation of all artistic endeavour. Shakespeare's work is about rhetoric, and his relationship to rhetoric seems paradoxical. His style is excessively polysemous, illusive, resonant, and complex — and in some ways, atypical of early modern poetry. Most of his contemporaries followed Cicero's teachings. They were faithful to one of three styles — grand, middle or low — roughly corresponding to the tragic, the dramatic, and the comic. These styles were consistently utilized separately in relation to the three different genres. Shakespeare, on the other hand, was influenced by the Greek rhetorician Hermogenes of Tarsus, adopting many different styles *in one passage*. He also utilized many different genres simultaneously, often swiftly moving from one to another. Finally, Shakespeare's characters eloquently argue on both sides of any issue. It is difficult to classify any of his characters as purely good or evil; most come in shades of grey. Even Iago — who is the closest thing to the devil himself in Shakespeare's work — is relentlessly articulate, charming, and at moments even vaguely sympathetic.

Shakespeare was a master craftsman of connotative language and rhetorical art. He was more interested in the process of the search for truth than in providing answers to questions. He would agree with Lessing, the 18th century dramaturge who was, not coincidentally, one of the great early champions of Shakespeare's work: "Science cannot solve the ultimate mystery of nature ... the true value of man is not determined by his possession, supposed or real, of the Truth, but rather by his sincere exertion to get to what lies behind the truth" (460-61).[5]

Though Shakespeare's attitude to specific issues is difficult to discern, his philosophical bent is clear. The form of his work indicates he believed that aesthetics was not just a philosophy, but that it should replace philosophy completely. For an aesthete, the only reality is art; the only truth is a lie. The aesthete has a very tentative relationship with the material world. Skepticism is a necessary corollary of this belief. This skepticism is by nature somewhat mystical. Shakespeare did not believe art was meant to teach, but to provide us — not only with a release of human emotion — but a deep connection to something beyond the quotidian real. He believed that poetry offered a catharsis for both the spectator and the poet alike. For Shakespeare, art was therapy — but nothing like a helpful hour you might spend with a sympathetic social worker. Instead, Shakespeare insists on confronting the spectator with impossible situations, impossible choices, and impossible people. He believes in asking unanswerable questions. The fictional dilemmas Shakespeare creates trigger enormous anxiety in his audiences. But, paradoxically, when we refuse easy answers, we discover a certain peace, one that can come only from resting within the knowledge that the enigma called life is something we may never truly understand.

This might sound complex, opaque, and pretentious. It is certainly complex and opaque. But Shakespeare would argue — 'so is life.' Was Shakespeare a philosopher/aesthete who believed art was dangerously powerful magic? Absolutely. He immersed himself in the works of the Roman skeptic Sextus Empiricus and was a passionate reader of the Greek rhetorician Gorgias and the Roman poet Ovid. Shakespeare was not only naturally brilliant, but more well read than anyone — then or now. Was Shakespeare an aristocrat, educated at the Inns of Court, with access to the library of William Cecil, Lord Baron Burghley (the greatest library in early modern England)? Was Shakespeare the Earl of Oxford?

Not necessarily. And to enjoy this book, you needn't think that Shakespeare was Edward de Vere. But you must open yourself to the notion that Shakespeare had the giants of Greek and Roman literature at his fingertips — and that he had the education, intelligence, and intellectual discernment to be inspired by them.

You must believe this — because the proof is in his work.

Endnotes

[1] Tannahill, Jordan. *Theatre of the Unimpressed*. Coach House Books, 2015.

[2] McGilchrist, Iain. *The Master and His Emissary.* Yale University Press, 2009.

[3] McGilchrist, Iain.

[4] Wilde, Oscar. *Intentions: The Decay of Lying, Pen Pencil and Poison, The Critic as Artist, The Truth of Masks.* Brentano's, 1905.

[5] McGilchrist, Iain. *The Master and His Emissary.* Yale University Press, 2009.

Chapter One: Skepticism

Was Shakespeare a skeptic? Most critics comment on how hopeless it is to confirm his opinion about anything. Others take sides. Phyllis McBride tells us Walt Whitman believed Shakespeare's sympathies lay with the aristocracy — that his works "exalt that principle of caste which we Americans have come on earth to destroy."[1] Ulysses' romanticization of the feudal caste system in *Troilus and Cressida* appears to support this idea: "The heavens themselves, the planets and this centre / Observe degree, priority and place, / Insisture, course, proportion, season, form, / Office and custom, in all line of order" (1.3. 89-92).[2] But Franco Moretti claims Shakespeare's tragedies call for the destruction of the aristocracy; the histories and tragedies are "posing the question of whether a cultural foundation of power is still possible ... In the tragedies, sovereign power has become instead an insoluble problem" (64).[3] Moretti's opinion makes some sense, but one could easily play devil's advocate with it. Perhaps Shakespeare wrote about the demise of the aristocracy because he loved aristocrats so terribly much. After all, his sympathy for crumbling monarchs (from Richard II on) is 'bottomless.' Is the search for Shakespeare's opinion on anything merely an endless, hopeless game?

But if Shakespeare was a skeptic, his work might be quite pointedly 'pointless.' P. Walsh defines isossthenia, the central concept of skepticism, as "the practice of placing arguments and counterarguments in contact with each other in order to show the impotence of both" (28).[4] The result is the 'epoche' — a dearth of belief — considered a positive end in itself. The *Stanford Encyclopedia of Philosophy* speaks of Sextus Empiricus, the great Roman advocate for the Greek skeptic Pyhrro: "The Pyrrhonian skeptic has the skill of finding for every argument an equal and opposing argument, a skill whose employment will bring about suspension of judgment on any issue which is considered by the skeptic, and ultimately, tranquility".[5] Sextus' attitudes to truth were very different from the attitudes of Plato and Aristotle. He held there should be no dogma, only questions.

Certainly a skeptical attitude seems plausible for a writer who confuses us with so many points of view. As we are generally creatures of the enlightenment — deeply rooted in Plato and Aristotle — skepticism has been (at least up until recently) largely forgotten. But in the 16th century, as traditional ideologies crumbled, skeptical philosophy stepped in to take their place. The obliteration of the Roman Catholic Church in England left room for the onset of the Reformation, which was, in itself, a new kind of skepticism: long-standing, firmly held beliefs were shattered. William H. Hamlin says, "I propose, moreover, that ... scepticism [sic] ... owe(s its) ... existence in late Renaissance Europe primarily to the period's unprecedented ideological controversies" (10).[6] The early modern skeptical door opened for only a brief period; it was closed by Descartes only thirty-seven years after, and finally buried by The Enlightenment.

Leonie Pawlita claims Descartes' most famous dictum was written in response to skepticism. Descartes defined 'genius malignus' as a furious doubt that could come to any man at any time, causing him to muse on whether or not the world he sees before him is the real one. Descartes invents this malignant force in order to triumph over it; his answer to this paralyzing uncertainty is 'I think, therefore I am':

> The quest for certainty, the symptom of the time, so to speak, became more and more virulent particularly in the first half of the seventeenth century. Descartes' project is only the most conspicuous symptom of the attempt to overcome skepticism with the intention to establish a firm basis of certainty of knowledge, a philosophical foundation for the scientific exploration of the world (105-106).[7]

Most well-educated English Renaissance men had encountered Sextus Empiricus' version of Pyrrhonian skepticism. Ben Jonson was clearly acquainted with his work. As Hamlin tells us: "Sextus' *Outlines of Pyrrhonism* and *Against the Mathematicians* were finally published in the mid-sixteenth century" (3),[8] and "skepticism was perceived, at both Oxford and Cambridge, as an intellectual orientation with which students needed to reckon, and about which they were therefore expected to possess some degree of familiarity" (48).[9]

Scholars have long acknowledged that Shakespeare and Thomas Nashe must have known each other; perhaps it is no surprise that they expressed similar skeptical sentiments. Hamlin suggests Nashe's *Terrors of The Night* was "composed by a writer clearly conscious of Sextus' ideas" (70).[10] Bronson Feldman quotes Nashe's direct reference to Sextus Empiricus: "our opinion (as Sextus Empiricus affirmeth) gives the name of good or ill to everything" (139).[11] Bronson notes that Nashe's sentiment echoes Hamlet's famous observation — "for there is nothing either good or bad but thinking makes it so" (2.2. 268-70),[12] and also reminds us of Nashe's prologue to *Summer's Last Will and Testament*, which warns those too intent on discovering a work's literal meaning: "Moralizers, you that wrest a never meant meaning out of everything, applying all things to the present time, keep your attention for the common stage: for here are no quips in characters for you to read" (139).[13] Shakespeare says it more succinctly in the subtitle of *12th Night* — '*What You Will.*'

Shakespeare had undoubtedly *heard* of skepticism. However the ideas expressed by the characters in Shakespeare's plays are sometimes skeptical, and sometimes not. So instead, we must turn to the form of his work to discern his intentions. Shakespeare's fondness for a certain kind of wordplay cements his intentions; for how are we to understand the meaning of a work so replete with puns, work that revels in polysemous invention — but most of all, that is so steeped in paradox? John Lyly was Shakespeare's contemporary (and Edward de Vere's secretary). The most stunning formal similarity between Lyly and Shakespeare is their affection for paradox. It's unfortunate that so few scholars have made a meaningful connection between them — because their use of paradox is intrinsically connected to skepticism.

At times Euphues (the lead character in Lyly's novels) battles with his own wit — a wit which would have been considered corrupt and Italianate by English readers. By the end of the story he is a man isolated — writing against the excesses of rhetorical abundance and coming to no perceivable conclusion. As Mentz points out, Lyly's *The Anatomy of Wit* "ends up with four pages of balanced antitheses that add up to exactly nothing" (162).[14] Like most critics, Mentz thinks that Lyly's work lacks profundity. For this reason scholars have been reluctant to note similarities between his work and Shakespeare's.

However, critic Jonas Barish insists that to separate the style and subject matter of Lyly's work "interferes even with subjective descriptions of style, interferes still more with any effort to get at the heart of a writer's artistic universe, where style and meaning interpenetrate" (15-16).[15] Barish believes that the use of paradox is not only endemic to Lyly and Shakespeare, but has profound implications for both authors. He speaks of a type of paradox which "asserts the actual co-existence of contrary opposites in one phenomenon" (19).[16]:

> Lyly prefers the kind of natural curiosity that challenges common sense [...] the result of overthrowing it so many scores of times is to establish a new assumption, a kind of grand paradox emerging from the countless minor ones; that things are not what they seem, that like allies itself with unlike, that fair and foul, precious and worthless, hurtful and beneficent co-exist in perpetual and inseparable intimacy. And this whole system of contradictions is Lyly's way of expressing the perpetual ambiguities of human sentiment, and above all of the most ambiguous of all human sentiments, love ... The lover, freezing in flames and burning in ice, joyful in grief and grievous in joy, becomes merely *e pluribus unus*, the final and most perfect expression of a universal paradox. (24)[17]

Barish thinks that Lyly's work was — for whatever reason — a literary experiment in a style that Shakespeare was later to perfect: "a style that needed only the further flexibility and modulation brought to it by Shakespeare to become an ideal dramatic prose" (35).[18]

It is not only the verbal display. Shakespeare's experiments in genre hint at his philosophical leanings. Hamlin asserts that the form of *Troilus and Cressida* — routinely characterised as either comical tragedy or tragical comedy — offers proof of Shakespeare's skepticism:

> Sextus would have appreciated the degree to which the flourishing of Elizabethan tragedy tacitly interrogated the generic descriptions promulgated by Aristotle and prescriptively endorsed by neoclassical orthodoxy. I suspect that he would have delighted in the formal indeterminacies of *Troilus and Cressida* (7).[19]

It's worth mentioning that Hamlin not only labels the form of *Troilus and Cressida* skeptical, but notes that the subject matter of the play is skeptical too. The play's central conflicts revolve around perceptual confusion — a fundamental principle of skeptical thought, explained by Pawlita here: "The skeptics' argumentative repertoire ... emphasize that sensory perception cannot provide a basis for certain knowledge" (81).[20] In other words, the skeptic questions the ontological and epistemological power of the senses; and questions their ability to reveal not only what is good and beautiful, but what is true.

The soldiers in the Roman camp in *Troilus and Cressida* debate endlessly what a hero is. Ajax and Achilles compete for the title; much misperception is based on whether their outside appearance and actions — i.e., their boasting, and the strength of their physical bodies — makes them prime candidates. The Trojan scenes mirror this perceptual confusion, but here the issue is love. After Troilus catches Cressida flirting with Diomedes, Troilus no longer knows who she is: "This she? No, this is Diomed's Cressida ... this is, and is not, Cressid" (5.2.166-75).[21] Finally, Cressida's betrayal places *all* perception under suspicion, as her betrayal 'doth invert th' attest of eyes and ears, / As if those organs had deceptious functions, / Created only to calumniate" (5.2.128–30).[22]

The hero's similar perceptual cul-de-sacs contribute to the central dilemma in *Hamlet* — highlighted in his first scene when Hamlet scolds his mother: "'Seems', madam?

Nay, it is. I know not 'seems'" (1.2.79-80).[23] Hamlet suspects that his mother and uncle are guilty of killing his father, but he is not sure. The ghost of his father tells him in no uncertain terms to kill Claudius, but the ghost can be seen and heard only by Hamlet alone. Hamlet cannot trust his five senses; mysterious forces attack his eyes and ears. The deceptiveness of appearances is also the subject of Hamlet's infamous 'madness,' as he himself becomes living proof that it is quite impossible to discern someone's inner sensibility by merely observing their behaviour.

How can we take the skeptical notion of perceptual confusion seriously? How, in fact, does the skeptic live? Take the rather ordinary question: should I bring an umbrella to work? Some people trust meteorological predictions; but, such people have also been known to get wet. The skeptic's answer is to reject logic (meteorological facts) because a logical argument may justify any opinion, and for every scientist who predicts rain, another can prove the opposite. The skeptic looks out the window. If it is cloudy or rainy he will probably carry an umbrella, and if it is sunny, he probably will not. The skeptics trust their hunches — which are based on appearances — but they know that appearances are simply that; they do not *mean* anything; they do not express a deeper reality. Appearances, for the skeptic, are a lie that we accept — for daily convenience — as truth.

The *Stanford Encyclopedia of Philosophy* tells us that a student of the skeptical atomist Democritus (Anaxarchus of Abdera) "likened existing things to a stage painting," and was even quoted as saying "all the world's a stage painting."[24] This phrase bears a remarkable resemblance to Jaques' oft-quoted line from Shakespeare's *As You Like It*: "All the world's a stage" (2.7.146).[25] The atomist Monismus shared Democritus' concept of reality as a stage painting, inferring that such a notion has moral and pragmatic implications; i.e., that "all is vanity."[26] In other words, we may be making up what reality is, and we should be wary of the self-centred assumption that we know so very much about anything at all. Perceptual confusion is the primary subject matter of Shakespeare's work — it is not just *Hamlet* and *Troilus and Cressida* — but every play and poem eventually circles around the question of the relationship between appearances and reality.

Why does Lucrece digress at length (for some thirty stanzas) on a painting of the Trojan war, right after she has been brutally raped by Tarquin? One can be forgiven for thinking that the subject matter of Lucrece is not rape, but the deceptiveness of art. She describes the Trojan painting as something to be wary of, as a misleading representation that is dangerously close to the real: "For such imaginary work was there, / Conceit deceitful, so compact, so kind, / That for Achilles' image stood his spear / Gripped in an armed hand, himself behind / Was left unseen, save to the eye of mind" (1422-26).[27] But art as deception is only one side of the argument; Shakespeare is not proselytizing *against* art. For Lucrece also praises the artist for surpassing reality, as in the painting: "a thousand lamentable objects there / In scorn of Nature, Art gave lifeless life" (1373-74).[28]

In paradoxical, skeptical fashion, Shakespeare is clearly interested in art as a dangerous deception, and yet there is one thing, and one thing alone, that might cause us to think Shakespeare is on the side of art. He is dedicated to creating wondrous, fantastical fictional worlds that seduce us into thinking they are real. Shakespeare's work is a humongous lie that seduces us into willing belief. The liar's paradox hides at the centre of all Shakespeare's work; he is a confirmed liar who tries to persuade us — through the beauty of his work — that he is not lying. Ultimately, he wishes for us to turn to the experience of poetry — because it will provide us with the skeptic's desired 'epoche' — a moment of blissful contemplation.

Shakespeare's obvious affinity with skeptical philosophy is not merely interesting; it has wide ranging implications for understanding his work. Shakespeare was undoubtedly reading Greek and Roman philosophy in the original languages, and his wide ranging reading would not only have offered him knowledge, but precipitated his own particular philosophical stance. It is not entirely clear why Shakespeare scholars seem so reluctant to associate Shakespeare with a particular philosophical school. Perhaps it's because to associate his work with skepticism has deep philosophical implications for how we read his work and perceive it. And such implications may challenge, fundamentally, scholarly research into the bard.

Both Greek and Roman philosophies were dominated by a philosophical divide between skepticism and foundationalism. Simply put, the skeptics assumed reality was a 'stage painting' and that we cannot trust our senses to understand what it is; there is no 'there' there. Foundationalists, on the other hand, believed that there is a reality that we can see, and must observe. The ancient Greek philosophy of Skepticism existed in direct opposition to the Eleatic school (Parmenides, Zeno of Elea and Melissus). Skepticism formed the basis for sophism (inaugurated by the first sophist, Gorgias — of him much will be said later) and Eleatic philosophy laid the foundation for Plato and Aristotle, and eventually, the Enlightenment. For modern Shakespeare critics, it won't do for Shakespeare to be a skeptic or sophist as this would put his work at odds with the very foundation of western post-enlightenment philosophy. But unfortunately, Shakespeare's work is inspired by an antiquated philosophical position that is directly opposed to our own. And this may be one of the many reasons his work is so powerful as well as somewhat inexplicable.

The fundamental quarrel between the skeptical/atomistic/epicurean approach to life and the Eleatic/Platonist/Aristotelian view lies in their different attitudes to certainty. Plato and Aristotle both believed that there was 'a truth' somewhere. (Plato found his reality through shadows on a wall; but nevertheless, there was a 'there' there.) Skeptics, on the other hand, believed that the universe (and therefore reality) was not identifiable or easily understood, and that we must content ourselves with the notion that it is merely an appearance — and then set about enjoying it. That Shakespeare was drawn to skepticism means that he was not only on the side of the sophists, but of the atomists and the epicureans.

Epicureanism and Skepticism are linked by their connection to the ancient Greek philosophy of Atomism, and by their opposition to the Eleatic school. Democritus — along with another skeptic, Pyrrho — knew (as the *Stanford Encyclopedia* tells us) that "[i]n truth we know nothing; for truth is in the depths."[29] Democritus invented Atomism, which later became the foundation for Epicureanism. Epicurus used Atomism as an excuse to promote aestheticism: the enjoyment of life and beauty. As *Stanford* says again: "Epicurus was less troubled by any such epistemological uncertainties because of his emphasis on the value of atomist theory for teaching us how to live the untroubled and tranquil life."[30] Indeed, the skeptical atomist Democritus is often referred to as the 'cheery' philosopher or the 'laughing philosopher.'

Certain Shakespeare critics have dipped their toes into the uncharted waters of these unpopular and somewhat scandalous branches of Greek philosophy by daring to suggest that Shakespeare may have been an epicurean. Jonathan Bate says: "In an intellectual biography of Shakespeare called *Soul of the Age* (2008), I suggested that if we were to pin any philosophical label on the myriad-minded Bard, 'Shakespeare the Epicurean' would be about as good as we could get."[31] Bate cites this 'epicurean' passage from *The Two Noble Kinsmen*:

> O you heavenly charmers,
> What things you make of us! For what we lack
> We laugh, for what we have are sorry, still
> Are children in some kind. Let us be thankful
> For that which is, and with you leave dispute
> That are above our question. (5.4.154-59).[32]

The link between Epicureanism and Atomism has to do with flux and change. For both philosophies, the world is in a constant state of transformation. Scott Consigny suggests that, for atomists, "reality is not to be found in the artificial rationally constructed domain that Parmenides says exists outside of time and place, but is [...] constantly changing in a condition of ceaseless flux" (43).[33] It is impossible to speak about flux and change in the Renaissance without thinking of Ovid, as flux and change are a pervasive theme in Shakespeare's work. It has long been clear that Ovid's *Metamorphoses* was a primary source for Shakespeare; his plays and poems allude to Ovid more often than any other poet.

We know Shakespeare had heard of Atomism because he references it several times. In the 'Queen Mab' speech from *Romeo and Juliet* Mercutio intones: "She is the fairies' midwife, and she comes / In shape no bigger than an agate stone / On the forefinger of an alderman / Drawn with a team of little atomi" (1.4.59-63).[34] In *As You Like It*, Celia observes, "It is as easy to count atomies as to resolve the propositions of a lover" (3.2.228).[35] Atoms are referred to obliquely in *The Merchant of Venice*: "There's not the smallest orb that thou behold'st / But in his motion like an angel sings" (5.1.68-69).[36] Lucretius was the Roman philosopher whose work (inspired by Epicurean Atomism) was discovered by Renaissance scholars. Stephen Greenblatt claims that "[t]he author of *Romeo and Juliet* shared his interest in Lucretian materialism with Spenser, Donne, Bacon, and others. He could have discussed it with his fellow-playwright Ben Jonson, whose own signed copy of *On the Nature of Things* has survived and is today in the Houghton Library, at Harvard."[37]

The atomists, like Shakespeare, were singularly obsessed with infinity and nothingness. Jonathan Pollack notes that in Atomism "everything is the result of fortuitous assemblages of atoms, but for these atoms to have chances of meeting and joining with one another, their existence must be eternal, their form immutable, their number infinite and their movement incessant, unlike the finite universe and the concentrate cosmic spheres postulated by the Aristotle/Thomas world picture, the atoms move about in an 'infinite deal of nothing' (126)."[38] Conveniently, 'An infinite deal of nothing' is a quotation from Shakespeare's *Merchant of Venice*. Shakespeare often employed the word 'nothing' as a metaphor. Richard II says: "I am unking'd by Bolingbroke / And straight am nothing: but what'er I be, / Nor I not any man but man is / With nothing shall be pleased, till he be pleased / With being nothing" (5.1.36-41).[39] The word 'nothing' appears thirty-four times in *King Lear*, and Hamlet uses the word twenty-eight times.

'Nothing' is significant because it is a purely imaginary concept and unavailable to our perceptions. We cannot see it; we can only imagine it. The atomistic universe is also a universe of 'nothing.' Carla Mazzio suggests that this is where King Lear lives: "If atomism conjured invisible materialism beyond the reaches of the senses, Shakespeare makes spectacular, palpable and moving the very drama of nothing, the drama of unseen seeds of being, of infinite divisibility and emptiness" (243).[40]

The Eleatics, and Aristotle — unlike Shakespeare — rejected the idea of an imaginary 'nothing.' The number zero — although not the same as nothing — is related to it, and during The Middle Ages '0' existed only in the Arabic numeric system. It was not allowed into the western numerical system until the early modern period — when it was still considered both mathematically and metaphysically threatening. 'Nothing' and 'zero' were beyond the senses; they were imagined worlds. Shakespeare was obsessed with all things imaginary. Many of his plays are set in imagined places, and characters ponder dreams, madness, and art, all the things that are not dreamt of in 'Horatio's philosophy.' And more importantly, they offer the possibility of another reality that supersedes this one.

Further, there is quite a significant connection between Nicholas Hill — 'the English atomist' — and Edward de Vere. If we follow the connection, it's clear that an atomist may very well have been Shakespeare's friend. Very little is actually known about Nicholas Hill; most of it is conjecture. Hill's one complete book *Philosophia Epicurea, Democritiana, Theophrastica* is a collection of aphorisms, many of which seem, on the face of it, to be irrelevant to the book's subject (philosophy). Historian Hugh Trevor-Roper says Hill "was an early advocate of a Copernican solar system, the first Englishman to advance the theory of a plurality of worlds, the first of the moderns publicly to preach Epicurean atomism" (2).[41] Trevor-Roper tells us Hill's writing style was deliberately obscure (as Shakespeare's often was). Hill wrote: "'[T]he name of Lucifer' — that is, of the Light-bringer — 'is damned'"

(3).[42] Trevor-Roper continues: "As a philosopher, he was of the School of Night, not Enlightenment: of Hermes Trismegistus, not of Francis Bacon" (3),[43] and: "[I]t is the universe of Giordano Bruno, a universe in which the cold mechanical atomic theory which Bruno had found in Lucretius is extended to infinity and animated with divine life. Like Bruno, Hill repudiates the old Aristotelean universe entirely" (31).[44]

One clear connection between Hill and de Vere is the philosopher Cardanus (also known as Cardeno). Trevor-Roper describes Cardanus as "a precursor of Bruno and Hill" (4).[45] When de Vere was twenty-three years old, he commissioned the publication of Thomas Bedingford's translation of Cardeno's *Cardanus Comforte*, offering an introduction praising Cardano's philosophy. Nicholas Hill has been linked with Edward de Vere in other ways. Aubrey wrote that Hill was actually de Vere's secretary (but of this there is no actual proof). Other stories — even more apocryphal — associate the two. These concern farting.

Trevor-Roper tells us John Donne created a fanciful list of imaginary books by bizarre authors. He attributed one particularly odd, imagined work to Hill: "'Cardanus de nullibietate crepitus' — Cardanus on the non-existence in space of the Fart" (4).[46] DeVere was also associated with farting — Aubrey tells the famous (perhaps fictional) story of de Vere farting before the Queen. Apparently the fart was an accident due to de Vere's low bow. According to legend, Elizabeth punished de Vere by exiling him to the European continent for seven years. Upon his return, Aubrey alleges that the Queen remarked — 'My Lord, I had forgot the Fart.'

The story may simply be one of the many early modern attacks on de Vere's character; and, of course, these 'fart' stories may be related to the fact that both de Vere and Hill were known for their love of obscenity. But there may be a philosophical reason to link Hill and de Vere with farting. Trevor-Roper tells us that the philosopher Robert Burton included in the fifth edition of his *Anatomy of Melancholy* a new chapter entitled 'A Digression on Air,' and in this, he speculated on the possibility of a plurality of worlds and quoted, with implicit approval, Hill's expression of that doctrine: "'sperabundus exspecto innumerabilium mundorum in aeternitate perambulationem' — why should not an infinite cause (as God is) produce infinite effects?" (6).[47] A fart, of course, might be described as a 'digression on air.'

So, is it possible that de Vere and Hill were known for their lofty and abstruse atomistic philosophizing about the plurality of worlds? Yes. Why? Because Shakespeare was a skeptical, epicurean atomist who assaulted us over and over again with his theory that art — despite (or perhaps because) it is a lie — is, in actuality, more real than life itself, and offers a kind of ineffable, ecstatic escape to a fantastical place that exists only in the poetic imaginary.

Theodor Adorno (1903-1969) is the modern philosopher whose aestheticism most resembles Shakespeare's. Interestingly, Adorno wrote much music criticism (Shakespeare often compares poetry and rhetoric to music), and has often been criticized for being devoted to 'high art' (which for many, means Shakespeare). Adorno is opposed to art with obvious, relevant, political content; art that deals with 'issues' — art that intends to morally improve us. Adorno said art about the Holocaust was — however well intentioned — ultimately futile and impotent, and destined to fail at precipitating change. He thought that it was Samuel Beckett who wrote most persuasively about the Holocaust, *precisely because Beckett never mentions the Holocaust in his work*. Instead, Adorno insists that the form of Beckett's work is the most eloquent argument against the devastating cruelty of fascism.

In fact, Adorno is suspicious of any sort of art which moralizes, because he states: "Under fascism too, no atrocity was committed without a moral veneer" (193).[48] He said: "However sublime, thoughts can never be much more than one of the materials of art" (182).[49] Artists should not imitate our world or create ideal worlds, just new ones. The artist does not create perfect societies, or describe moral situations in order to teach us, but simply creates alternate universes — and we cannot help but compare our own universe to the imaginary ones.

Adorno cites *The Sorrows of Young Werther*. Goethe's novel was an early 19th century, sentimental, dark, romantic fairy tale. A young man falls in love with a married woman. When she rejects him, he takes his own life. Because of the world it created — not because of any stated theme in the text —*The Sorrows of Young Werther* offered a critique of middle class culture without expressing it in so many words. For Adorno, the best art is 'hermetic' or 'autonomous', which means that it creates its meaning through its structure: "The moment of true volition, however, is mediated through nothing other than the form of the work itself" (194).[50]

Shakespeare created hermetically sealed worlds — the characters often act in ways that people do not in real life. For instance, they fall in love with an ass, they chat with ghosts, they disbelieve witches' predictions that prove to be frighteningly true, or they are mistaken for their differently gendered twin. The stories have no morals, and the characters' warring ideas are endlessly contradictory. The form of these works shift from comedy to tragedy and back again; the words bump into each other — like 'little atomies' — and transform into each other, exchanging unstable meanings. But within the fantastical worlds Shakespeare creates, everything *somehow makes sense*. Shakespeare's plays — despite their fantastical unlikeliness — seem psychologically true, and though the action may at times *seem* 'realistic,' what seals them hermetically from the outside world is their imperviousness to our attempts to interpret them. We can never ask, 'What is the lesson?' of a Shakespeare play, because we might as well ask, 'What is the lesson of life?' And, for Shakespeare, art is more real than reality, more true than truth.

Endnotes

1 McBride, Phylliss. https://whitmanarchive.org/criticism/current/encyclopedia/entry_329.html (4th paragraph).

2 Shakespeare, William. *Troilus and Cressida.* (New Folger's ed.), Washington Square Press/Pocket Books, 2021.

3 Moretti, Franco. *Signs Taken for Wonders: On the Sociology of Literary Forms.* Generic, 1983.

4 Walsh, P. *Skepticism, Modernity and Critical Theory.: Critical Theory in Philosophical Context.* Palgrave Macmillan, 2005.

5 "Sextus Empiricus." *Stanford Encyclopedia of Philosophy.* https://plato.stanford.edu/entries/sextus-empiricus/ Accessed December 29, 2021.

6 Hamlin, William. T*ragedy and Skepticism in Shakespeare's England*. Palgrave, 2005.

7 Pawlita, Leonie "Dream And Doubt: Skepticism In Shakespeare's Hamlet And Calderón's La Vida Es Sueño" *Theatre Cultures within Globalising Empires: Looking at Early Modern England and Spain,* (Joachim Küpper and Leonie Pawlita), De Gruyter, 2018.

8 Hamlin, William. *Tragedy and Skepticism in Shakespeare's England*. Palgrave, 2005.

9 Hamlin, William. *Tragedy and Skepticism in Shakespeare's England.*

10 Hamlin, William. *Tragedy and Skepticism in Shakespeare's England.*

[11] Feldman, Bronson. *Hamlet Himself.* iUniverse, 2010.

[12] Shakespeare, William. *Hamlet.* (New Folger's ed.), Washington Square Press/Pocket Books, 1992.

[13] Feldman, Bronson. *Hamlet Himself.* iUniverse, 2010.

[14] Mentz, Steve. "Escaping Italy: From Novella to Romance in Gascoigne and Lyly." *Studies in Philology*, Vol. 101, No. 2.

[15] Barish, Jonas "The Prose Style of John Lyly." *ELH*, Vol. 23, No. 1.

[16] Barish, Jonas "The Prose Style of John Lyly."

[17] Barish, Jonas "The Prose Style of John Lyly."

[18] Barish, Jonas "The Prose Style of John Lyly."

[19] Hamlin, William. *Tragedy and Skepticism in Shakespeare's England*. Palgrave, 2005.

[20] Pawlita, Leonie. "Dream And Doubt: Skepticism In Shakespeare's Hamlet And Calderón's La Vida Es Sueño" *Theatre Cultures within Globalising Empires: Looking at Early Modern England and Spain,* (Joachim Küpper and Leonie Pawlita), De Gruyter, 2018.

[21] Shakespeare, William. *Troilus and Cressida.* (New Folger's ed.), Washington Square Press/Pocket Books, 2021.

[22] Shakespeare, William. *Troilus and Cressida.*

[23] Shakespeare William. *Hamlet*. (New Folger's ed.), Washington Square Press/Pocket Books, 2021 1992.

[24] "Ancient Skepticism." *Stanford Encyclopedia of Philosophy.* https://plato.stanford.edu/entries/skepticism-ancient/ Accessed December 29, 2021

[25] Shakespeare, William. *As You Like It.* (New Folger's ed.), Washington Square Press/Pocket Books, 2015.

[26] "Ancient Skepticism." *Stanford Encyclopedia of Philosophy.* https://plato.stanford.edu/entries/skepticism-ancient/ Accessed December 29, 2021

[27] Shakespeare, William. *The Complete Sonnets and Poems.* Oxford University Press, 2002.

[28] Shakespeare, William. *The Complete Sonnets and Poems.*

[29] "Presocratic Philosophy." *Stanford Encyclopedia of Philosophy*. https://plato.stanford.edu/entries/presocratics/ Accessed December 29. 2021.

[30] "Ancient Atomism." *Stanford Encyclopedia of Philosophy* https://plato.stanford.edu/entries/atomism-ancient/ Accessed December 29 2021.

[31] Bate, Jonathan. "Shakespeare Was an Epicurean." *The New Republic* https://newrepublic.com/article/118664/shakespeares-debt-montaigne July 11, 2014.

[32] Shakespeare, William. *The Two Noble Kinsmen*. (New Folger's ed.), Washington Square Press/Pocket Books, 2010.

[33] Consigny, Scott. *Gorgias: Sophist and Artist.* University of South Carolina Press, 2001.

[34] Shakespeare, William. *Romeo and Juliet.* (New Folger's ed.), Washington Square Press/Pocket Books, 2004.

[35] Shakespeare, William. *As You Like It.* (New Folger's ed.), Washington Square Press/Pocket Books, 2015.

[36] Shakespeare, William. *The Merchant of Venice*. (New Folger's ed.), Washington Square Press/Pocket Books, 2014.

[37] Greenblatt, Stephen. "The Answer Man." *The New Yorker.* https://www.newyorker.com/magazine/2011/08/08/the-answer-man-stephen-greenblatt August 8, 2011.

[38] Pollock, Jonathan. "Of Mites and Motes." *Spectacular Science, Technology and Superstition in the Age of Shakespeare.* Edinburgh University Press, 2019.

[39] Shakespeare, William, *Richard II*. (New Folger's ed.), Washington Square Press/Pocket Books, 2014.

[40] Mazzio, Carla. "Scepticism and the Spectacular: On Shakespeare in an Age of Science." *Spectacular Science, Technology and Superstition in the Age of Shakespeare.* Edinburgh University Press, 2019.

[41] Trevor Roper, Hugh. *Catholics, Anglicans, and Puritans: Seventeenth-Century Essays*. University of Chicago Press,1987.

[42] Trevor Roper, Hugh. *Catholics, Anglicans, and Puritans.*

[43] Trevor Roper, Hugh. *Catholics, Anglicans, and Puritans.*

[44] Trevor Roper, Hugh. *Catholics, Anglicans, and Puritans.*

[45] Trevor Roper, Hugh. *Catholics, Anglicans, and Puritans*.

[46] Trevor Roper, Hugh. *Catholics, Anglicans, and Puritans*

[47] Trevor Roper, Hugh. *Catholics, Anglicans, and Puritans*

[48] Adorno, Theodor, "Commitment." *Aesthetics and Politics*, Verso, 1980.

[49] Adorno, Theodor, "Commitment."

[50] Adorno, Theodor, "Commitment."

Chapter Two: Gorgias

Pliny's tale of Zeuxis tells of a legendary Greek painter. He created such a realistic rendering of grapes on the vine that hungry birds pecked at it for food. In *Venus and Adonis*, the goddess's frustrated desire is compared to the plight of Zeuxis' birds, and Adonis' beauty — that Venus so lusts after — becomes a painting that seems to pulse with life: "E'en so she languisheth in her mishaps / As those poor birds that helpless berries saw" (601-04).[1] The notion that art might replace life is a dangerous one. Human life should be more valuable than art. However, Shakespeare was obsessed not only with the idea that art might be *mistaken* for life, but that it might *replace* it.

This notion speaks to a basic fear about art. In 1642, Richard Carpenter published an anti-Catholic treatise called *Experience, Historie, and Divinitie*. Carpenter's theme — favoured by 16th century English Protestants — was that music, vestments, ritual (and the Latin tongue itself) were Catholic agents of deception. The Catholic artist Michelangelo created works for the papistry that were amazingly lifelike. Land tells us that Carpenter not only says Michelangelo's depiction of the dying Christ "fools ignorant Catholics into believing they see life itself,"[2] but goes on to imply that Michelangelo tortured and killed the young man who modelled for him — "but he had the skill and genius required to resurrect the young man in his drawing. By virtue of the excellence of his art Michelangelo was allowed to escape punishment."[3]

The apocryphal tale refused to disappear. Land tells us the Sicilian painter Sussino said Michelangelo "used real nails to fix some poor man to a board and ... then pierced his heart with a lance in order to paint a Crucifixion."[4] In his novel *Justine* (1791), De Sade refers to the same story. "The importance of the tale," Land says, "is not so much that Michelangelo murdered a man, but that the artist had no conscience and was therefore free of remorse ... [The] typically Catholic Michelangelo considered his art — particularly the lifelike representation of nature — more important than the life of his model, and, in a sense, more important than nature itself."[5]

Land also reveals that Carpenter said art "will deceive you, with excuses, glosses, pretenses, professions, expressions, accusations. And he that suffers himself to be deceived by another is his foole."[6] On the contrary, Greek sophist Gorgias did not warn against being deceived; he taught that the fool is the one who is *not* deceived. Gorgias (483-375 B.C.) was arguably the first sophist. He is infamous due to Plato's misrepresentation of him in the *Dialogues* as an empty persuader, a manipulative wordsmith, a master of form with a dangerous lack of concern for content.

Gorgias practiced his art after 600 BC — sometimes referred to as the Greek enlightenment. McGilchrist tells us the period is marked by a growth of the frontal lobes which brought about "the beginnings of analytic philosophy, the coding of laws, the formalization of systematic bodies of knowledge. This requires the ability to stand back from and detach ourselves from the crowd" (259).[7] This was, in other words, the birthplace of reason, and the point at which reason and poetry emerged as fundamental opposites. But simply because 'reason' may have been 'discovered' by the Greeks after years of intuitive belief, Consigny quotes Pierre Vernant, asking us not to see this period as the "naive belief in the inevitable progress of society from the shadows of superstition toward the light of reason." (205)[8] Myths and art, too, are important, as they "provide individuals with a repertoire of binary oppositions, figurative analogies and examples or instructive cases for making sense of their experience" (205).[9]

Nevertheless, Plato excoriates Gorgias in *The Dialogues,* arguing that a sophist — the creator of myths — was simply a 'flatterer'. He said this because in order to dominate the public forum in Greece one had to be persuasive, and (as Bons notes) "sophists gave proof of their competence and virtuosity by presenting sample artistic speeches on a paradoxical theme, such as an encomium on salt, or on the bumble-bee" (39).[10] Plato and Aristotle dismissed them as snake-oil salesmen, auctioning their oratorical wares to the highest bidder.

It's no wonder Plato and Aristotle hated Gorgias, as his project was aimed directly at them. Gorgias wished for rhetoric not simply to compete with rational philosophy, but replace it. Gorgias rejected established, 'foundational' facts. In the manner of post-structuralists today, his methodology was to deconstruct what he considered philosophical lies masquerading as universal truths. As a master rhetor, he set out to extract and expose the techniques used by philosophers to manipulate their students.

Gorgias accused Socrates of cleverly posing as an ignorant, humble man; a naive, well-meaning innocent ambushed by reason, who accidentally stumbles upon the truth. Consigny says Gorgias saw the "Socratic strategy of self effacement as the clever pose of a person who wishes to conceal his foundationalist commitments" (193).[11] And, the Socratic philosophers criticized Gorgias in turn, because — "rather than promising to teach virtue, he laughs at others when he hears them so promising" (201).[12] However (Consigny continues), Gorgias managed to challenge the "slavish assent to dogmatic moral principles articulated by the deceptive and manipulative foundationalist thinker" (201).[13]

In order to replace philosophy with rhetoric, it was necessary for Gorgias to challenge reason. He does this in a frustrating and deeply controversial poem, *On Nature, or the Non-existent.* You may be forgiven for never having heard of it; G.B. Kerford reminds us that the work is not often read because of the "repulsive nature of its content" (3).[14] Kerferd summarizes Gorgias' most controversial and most misinterpreted work: "Nothing is. If it is, it is unknowable. If it is, and is knowable, it cannot be communicated to others" because "neither being nor not being exist" (5-6).[15] At any rate, it's difficult to know whether to take Gorgias' poem seriously, as it destroys the very foundation of ontological and epistemological understanding.

To get an idea of the kind of thinking that dominates Gorgias' essay — of the kind of merciless reasoning that does not allow the slightest pause for emotion, intuition, or even simply exhaustion, consider this description (from Damasio's *Descartes' Error*) of a patient who suffers damage to the right side of his brain (what can loosely be labelled the intuitive side) who is asked to decide on a date for his next appointment:

> For the better part of a half hour, the patient enumerated reasons for and against each one of the two dates ... he was now walking us through a tiresome cost-benefit analysis, an endless outlining and fruitless comparison of options and possible consequences. It took enormous discipline to listen to all of this without pounding on the table and telling him to stop. (193)[16]

Gorgias does much the same thing in his suffocating thesis. His arguments are bloodless, soulless, and counter-intuitive — but, nonetheless, ruthlessly logical. Kerferd quotes Gorgias' first principle: "If we say that it is possible for things not to be ... this leads us to the assertion that which is, is not, which is a contradiction and so impossible" (16).[17] Gorgias then makes reference to the ancient Greek philosopher Heraclitus who posited that *all things are in a constant state of change*: "If anything *is*, it would not be liable to change or movement. But things are liable to change and movement, therefore they *are not*" (23).[18] Once again, one can't help resenting Gorgias' reasoning somewhat, as he is relentlessly decimating something that we all instinctively value without question— our very existence.

Gorgias (paraphrased here by Johnstone) then goes on to observe that we can think about many things that are not real; just because we conceive of something doesn't mean it actually exists "since we can think about 'things' that don't exist outside the mind (such as 'a man flying, or chariots racing in the sea') and since we have no criterion by which to distinguish in thought the subjective from the objectively existing, we cannot know if what we think exists objectively actually does so" (273).[19]

Bakouakas quotes Kerferd, saying Gorgias' fundamental difficulty with reason is that everyone perceives the world differently; therefore, we can't communicate our reality to anyone else: "If it is known, no one could show it to another; because things are not words, and because no one thinks the same thing as another."[20] So, even if things *did* exist, we would not be able to talk about them — "words, according to Gorgias, could not be used to communicate information about objects outside us, so that the possibility of communication by means of logos [reason] is eliminated."[21]

Johnstone summarizes the conclusion to *On Nature or the Non-existent:* "To hold that nothing exists is to hold that nothing exists outside the sphere of human consciousness and that all realities are the products of perception and thought" (273).[22] *On Nature or the Non-existent* is clearly a challenge to the Eleatic philosophers Parmenides and Melissus, whose work laid the foundation for Aristotle and Plato, and who believed in exactly the opposite — that reality was (as Schiappa says) "ungenerated and unperishing, unchanging, stable, and forever" (25).[23]

After arriving at his unenviable conclusion, Gorgias' poem offers no plan for how we might conduct our lives. He writes no other poems on this particular subject, or in this particular manner. Perhaps it is no accident that the only surviving copy of *On Nature or the Non-existent* is a translation by Sextus Empiricus. Richard Bett says Sextus, when speaking of Gorgias, "does seem on firm ground when he claims ... a criterion of truth is effectively ruled out" (15).[24] Gorgias takes us through an exhaustive analysis only to arrive at a skeptical conclusion, but does not seem to offer us the tranquility offered by Sextus' skepticism.

But, alas, Gorgias does offer us a way out — he wishes to replace philosophy with rhetoric. Plato complained that it matters less *what* Gorgias said than *how* he said it — in the 'artfulness' of his work, because *On Nature or the Non-existent* is primarily a poem, not an essay. Consider its wordplay. Schiappa mentions the polysemous nature of Gorgias' conclusion: 'Nothing exists' could be interpreted in two ways. "Nothing," in this context, is ambiguous ... The difference is a matter of emphasis. One can say either that 'Nothing *exists*'... or that "*Nothing* exists" (25-26).[25] In other words, Gorgias might be simply telling us there is a thing called 'nothing,' or he might be making the much more pessimistic statement that the whole world is 'nothing.' His final conclusion is a rhetorical figure called amphiboly, an example of 'false reasoning' — that, predictably, Aristotle rejects in his *Sophistical Refutations*.

Gorgias' use of a rhetorical device at such a key moment is not merely a joke. Figurative language, wordplay, and metaphor are not just ornaments or amusements. In Gorgias' hands, they are vehicles of truth. McGilchrist asserts that it's a mistake to assume metaphors are merely ornamental, as "the loss of metaphor is a loss of cognitive content" (332). [26] Gorgias believed that poetry had a better chance of helping us to understand and perceive reality than denotative language. In fact, he believed all language was — to some degree — figurative. Consigny quotes Nietzsche who said that for the sophists, "tropes or figures of speech are not 'occasionally added to words but constitute their most proper nature' ... What is usually called language is actually all figuration" (77).[27]

According to Gorgias, even the most exacting language is inexact. Thus in *On Nature or The Non-existent*, Gorgias transforms the supposedly precise denotative language of logic into what he thinks it really is: the allusive connotative language of metaphor. He does this for two very radical reasons (according to Johnstone): "Gorgias' ostensible denial of objective reality as existent, knowable, or communicable had the effect of privileging speech itself as ontogenic (creating 'existence') and epistemic (creating knowledge)" (271).[28]

Gorgias' work appeared soon after the dawn of western reason, and Shakespeare's work appeared just before the Enlightenment. When Gorgias lived, Greek society was replacing the resonant fantasies of myth with the cold syllogisms of logic. When Shakespeare lived, Early Modern culture was clawing its way out of medieval religiosity into what would ultimately become science. Both Gorgias and Shakespeare sought to save metaphor because they believed it was *a tool of cognition.* Metaphor could offer understanding not available through reason. What is perceived in Shakespeare's poetry as both brilliant — and conversely as an obsession with stylistic detail, or an unwarranted excess – what is 'uber-poetic,' and can be perceived as overdone, or even just plain silliness, is there, as it was in Gorgias' work, for a specific reason. Gorgias' poetry is an attempt to come to terms with a confounding reality.

Gorgias and Shakespeare both believed there is a 'something' outside of ourselves, but it is not the kind of 'something' that can be described through rational thought or denotative language. Consigny is convinced that Gorgias used figurative language obsessively because he believed it was the only way to accurately represent the unrepresentable world: "Gorgias relentlessly experiments with the style of utterance in the hope of producing genuine novelty, because language can never accurately imitate what is real ... [and he] liked words that were strange, provincial, archaic or obsolete, and that require a glossary in order to be understood" (158).[29]

Shakespeare's poetry is self-consciously figurative, and calls attention to its own virtuosity. Many of the words and phrases Shakespeare used are, of course, not often heard today — but they were also rarely heard in early modern times. For both Shakespeare and Gorgias, style seems somewhat of a fetish — something that calls attention to itself. Both employ subtle rhymes, create new words, use epithets unsparingly, and choose bizarre and inscrutable metaphors. And, most significantly, both poets are addicted to paradox.

Consigny says Gorgias' frequent use of compound words was purposeful and meant to accent the fluidity of reality, as it "denies that single words must have on any given occasion, single meanings and ... it negates the notion that a word has meaning because it unequivocally names something in the world" (179-80).[30] Shakespeare had a similar affection for compound words. The list of those he invented includes (but is not limited to) dew-drop, earth-bound, full-hearted, high-blown, lack-luster, lily-livered, made-up, rope-trick (appropriately, meaning rhetoric), sad-eyed, sea-change, snail-paced, and time-honored.

Consigny says Gorgias frequently employed epithets — figures of speech in which a phrase is used to refer to some*one* or some*thing* without using its actual name. This is because the use of epithets reminds us that "things are not entities in the world that may simply be observed, [but] rather they are constructs, the product of human consciousness" (181).[31] Shakespeare's long list of epithets includes, from *Romeo and Juliet*, "star-crossed lovers" (Prologue. 6)[32] and "death-marked love" (Prologue. 9)[33] — for their tragic romance. There are also many instances in which a Shakespearean character curses another through epithet — like Gadshill in *Henry IV Part One,* who differentiates between his true friends and "mad mustachio purple-hued maltworms" (2.1.80).[34]

Gorgias and Shakespeare are both fond of complex and confusing metaphors. Aristotle called Gorgias' metaphors 'far-fetched,' and 'frigid.' Consigny notes that Aristotle singled out Gorgias' fanciful reprimand of a bird who defecated on him: "Shame on you Philomela; for if a bird did it there was no shame, but [it would have been] shameful for a maiden" (182-83).[35] Here Gorgias references the heavenly transformation of Philomena from maiden to bird. Thus Aristotle ridicules the metaphor as "far-fetched, as well as indecorous — 'He thus rebuked the bird by calling it what it once had been, not what it now was'" (183).[36]

Shakespeare's metaphors are often complicated, unlikely, and extreme. Cleopatra's hyperbolic description of Antony — though moving — is also somewhat absurd:

For his bounty,
There was no Winter in't; an Autumn 'twas
That grew the more by reaping: his delights
Were dolphin-like; they show'd his back above
The element they liv'd in: in his livery
Walk'd crowns and crownets.
Realms and islands were
As plates dropped from his pocket. (5.2.106-13)[37]

Here Shakespeare offers three different ways to look at Antony's 'bounty.' At least one of them is very strange indeed. For it is perhaps not unusual for Antony's lover to suggest that he was more like an autumn harvest than a winter scarcity — and to declare that islands dropped from his pockets is within the realms of hyperbole. But finally, to suggest that Antony's assets were 'dolphin-like' — the complex comparison being between the tendency for a dolphin's back to be revealed above water when it swims, and Antony's greatness to rise above all others — certainly stretches our imagination.

Gorgias' fondness for slant rhyme is also shared by Shakespeare, who sometimes uses both rhyming couplets and slant rhyme (half rhyme, or no rhyme at all). Critics have never been able to explain definitively why. The issue of rhyme in Shakespeare's work is so moot that *The Cambridge Companion to Shakespeare* equivocates "that Shakespeare sometimes uses half rhyme is indisputable ... how much he uses it is not clear" (58).[38] Here is an example: in Sonnet 90, the words 'taste' and 'last' are similar, but different — "If thou wilt leave me, do not leave me last, / When other petty griefs have done their spite, / But in the onset come; so I shall taste / At first the very worst of fortune's might" (9-12).[39] Slant rhyme is paradoxical; it puts a subtle emphasis on similarities that are somehow not the same, and points us to another shared obsession for both Shakespeare and Gorgias: a fondness for antithesis.

The five 'antithetical' figures of language favoured by Gorgias and Shakespeare (besides antithesis itself) include the 'likeness of sound' (found in slant rhyme), alliteration, repetition, arrangement of words in nearly equal periods, and puns. Consigny (quoting Untersteiner) says Gorgias' use of paradox "creates a simulacrum of the antithesis inherent in the nature of things thereby conveying through poetry what cannot be portrayed logically ... [he is] circumventing the impossibility of rational communication of the tragic nature of things by using an antithetical style" (155).[40]

It's not so much that Gorgias and Shakespeare employ antithesis more frequently than other poets, but by foregrounding it, Gorgias reminds us this particular figure of speech has a very special relationship to our perception of the world. Shakespeare's use of paradox — like Lily's — reminds us of the contradictory nature of love and life. But for Gorgias (and I would posit, for Shakespeare as well), the urge to think in paradoxes is not just a literary technique, but an existential compulsion. As Consigny says, "Man cannot escape the antithesis; his thoughts discover only the opposite poles in all proportions." (46).[41] Certainly when we think rationally, it's as if we are viewing the world only in one dimension. For life is *essentially* contradictory. We are born, and then we die. Or, as Samuel Beckett puts it, "They give birth astride of a grave, the light gleams an instant, then it's night once more" (89).[42]

Not only does Gorgias create the reality of our tenuous existence through paradox, but, according to Consigny, Gorgias conceived that "rather than antedating language, the very idea of what is 'real' emerges only within the specific discourses in which we use it" (80).[43] In other words, speaking about the world is the only way to understand it. Shakespeare references this notion in *Titus Andronicus*. Titus is tricked into cutting off his own hand. Suddenly he no longer wishes to say the word 'hands,' because — without the word — there would be no such thing as hands: "O, handle not the theme, to talk of hands ... / As if we should forget we had no hands / If Marcus did not name the word of hands" (3.2.29-33).[44] When a fly appears, Marcus, Titus' brother, swings at it with his knife, and Titus calls this a "deed of death done on the innocent" (3.2.56),[45] but when Marcus tells Titus the fly is black, Titus suddenly changes his tune, and the reality of the fly: "Yet, I think, we are not brought so low, / But that between us we can kill a fly / That comes in likeness of a coal-black Moor" (3.2.77-79).[46] The fly has no corporeal reality; it is whatever is assumed in speech.

We can't really understand Gorgias or Shakespeare until we understand Gorgias' obsession with the power of language. This is the focus of Gorgias' *Encomium of Helen*, where Gorgias takes up another unenviable cause, the defence of Helen of Troy. Helen, of heavenly ancestors, considered to be the most beautiful woman in the world, was seduced by the Trojan warrior Paris. Her subsequent abduction (or was it escape?) to Troy sparked the Trojan War. It would be an understatement to say that Helen was a controversial figure — in Greek culture she was depicted as both victim and adulteress. Was she seduced or kidnapped? Johnstone lists Gorgias' explanations for Helen's behaviour: "Either by will of Fate and decision of the gods and vote of Necessity did she do what she did, or by force seduced, or by words seduced, or by love possessed" (276).[47] Gorgias focuses on 'by words seduced' as the reason for her adultery — offering himself the chance to meditate on the supremely seductive nature of language.

Johnstone makes it clear that in *Encomium of Helen*, Gorgias is concerned with the hypnotic potency of rhetorical speech, with its pleasing sounds and seductive music. For Gorgias, words are magic. He gives "proof to the opinion [doxa] of [his] hearers': the 'agency of words' rests upon their power to 'beguile ... and persuade ... and alter [the soul] by witchcraft' ... a potency that 'is comparable to the power of drugs over the nature of bodies'" (276).[48] It is in *Encomium of Helen* that Gorgias says, "The one who ... is willingly deceived is 'wiser' (*sophoteros*) than the undeceived" (278).[49] Also (according to Johnstone), Gorgias in *Encomium of Helen* focuses on "the sense of the potency of speech in shaping opinion and thus in constructing the 'reality' in terms of which human beings must live their lives" (276).[50]

Gorgias goes even further when describing the power of language, suggesting that language *is* reality. *Encomium of Helen* implies not only that Helen was seduced by Paris, but that *the words themselves* constitute a kind of rape. In Shakespeare's *Venus and Adonis*, Adonis seems to be equating seductive words with physical assault, when he says to Venus, "I hate not love, but your device in love, / That lends embracements unto every stranger. / You do it for increase: O strange excuse, / When reason is the bawd to lust's abuse!" (790-93).[51] Consigny suggests that for Gorgias, "Language was actually action" (76)[52], anticipating J.L. Austin's 20th century concept of 'speech acts.' Austin claimed that certain phrases constitute actions. (The most obvious example — 'I do' — is spoken during the marriage ceremony.) Consigny tells us that in *Defence of Palamedes*, Gorgias' implies that 'words themselves become deeds" (76).[53]

Shakespeare's *Venus and Adonis* is a rhetorical argument in the form of a poem that does more than just confirm the persuasive power of human speech. The poem consists mainly of a series of monologues for Venus, in which she uses an intoxicating array of rhetorical arguments to seduce Adonis, including — like the narrator of *The Sonnets* — urging Adonis to take advantage of his beauty before it is wasted by time. Just as Paris seduced Helen through words that were, in effect, actions, Venus seems to be 'sexting' him: "Since I have hemm'd thee here / Within the circuit of this ivory pale, / I'll be a park, and thou shalt be my deer; / Feed where thou wilt, on mountain or in dale: / Graze on my lips; and if those hills be dry, / Stray lower, where the pleasant fountains lie" (229-234).[54]

Venus and Adonis is about the triumph of language over action, and imagination over reality. Venus fails in her attempt to seduce Adonis because he is distracted by his hunt of the blood-thirsty boar. She is jealous of the boar, because Adonis pays more attention to it than her, calling it "This sour informer, this bate-breeding spy, / This canker that eats up Love's tender spring" (665-66). [55] When the boar kills Adonis, it would seem that Venus' seduction has failed. But she conquers him with words. Shakespeare's description of Adonis' death is oddly sensuous, tender — even romantic: "Tis true, 'tis true; thus was Adonis slain: / He ran upon the boar with his sharp spear, / Who did not whet his teeth at him again, / But by a kiss thought to persuade him there; And nuzzling in his flank, the loving swine / Sheathed unaware the tusk in his soft groin" (1111-16).[56] Adonis, though dead, is raped by Venus in language.

For Shakespeare and Gorgias, speech has enormous potential for both good and evil; it can bewitch and intoxicate to any purpose. Words that we take as truth can be lies, and a master orator can persuade us anything is true. So how do we operate in a world where our reality can be changed simply through the words that are used to describe it? Well, as committed as Gorgias is to the notion that language creates reality, he is equally committed to reminding us that his own presentations are a lie. Gorgias thinks the man who is *not* deceived *is* a fool for a very important reason, because he — as Johnstone notes — "doesn't recognize the inherent deceptiveness in all language" (278).[57] What Gorgias urges is quite simply that we must take what anyone says — whether that person be a philosopher or a rhetor, with a grain of salt. If we are unconscious fools, then we will be completely susceptible to the 'dangers' of poetry as intoxicant. But, if we are willing to be self-conscious about it all, to be aware that all words are manipulative lies, then we will have the power to change our reality at will — and to believe that our reality changes according to which dream of reality we choose to believe at any given time. Gorgias' attitude to art is particularly modern, because it requires that an audience both believe desperately in a lie, and not believe it, at the same time. If we give this unique attitude to art its modern name it might intimidate us: some have called it 'camp.'

Endnotes

1 Shakespeare, William. "Venus and Adonis." *The Complete Sonnets and Poems*. Oxford University Press, 2002.

2 Land, Norman E. "Michelangelo, Giotto, and murder." *Explorations in Renaissance Culture,* vol. 32, no. 2, South Central Renaissance Conference, 2006. *link.gale.com/apps/doc/A241351972/AONE?u=guel77241&sid=bookmark-AONE&xid=c19e71a8*.

3 Land, Norman E. "Michelangelo, Giotto, and murder."

4 Land, Norman E. "Michelangelo, Giotto, and murder."

5 Land, Norman E. "Michelangelo, Giotto, and murder."

6 Land, Norman E. "Michelangelo, Giotto, and murder."

7 McGilchrist, Iain. *The Master and His Emissary*. Yale University Press, 2009.

[8] Consigny, Scott. *Gorgias: Sophist and Artist*. University of South Carolina Press, 2001.

[9] Consigny, Scott. *Gorgias: Sophist and Artist*. University of South Carolina Press, 2001.

[10] Bons, Jeroen A.E. "Gorgias the Sophist and Early Rhetoric." *A Companion to Greek Rhetoric.* (Ian Worthington, ed.) Blackwell, 2007.

[11] Consigny, Scott. *Gorgias: Sophist and Artist*. University of South Carolina Press, 2001.

[12] Consigny, Scott. *Gorgias: Sophist and Artist.*

[13] Consigny, Scott. *Gorgias: Sophist and Artist.*

[14] Kerferd, G.B. "Gorgias on Nature or That Which Is Not." *Phronesis.* Vol 1. No. 1, Nov., 1955.

[15] Kerferd, G.B. "Gorgias on Nature or That Which Is Not."

[16] Damasio, Antonio. *Descartes' Error*. Penguin, 2005

[17] Kerferd, G.B. "Gorgias on Nature or That Which Is Not." *Phronesis.* Vol 1. No. 1, Nov., 1955.

[18] Kerferd, G.B. "Gorgias on Nature or That Which Is Not."

[19] Johnstone, Christopher Lyle. "Sophistical Wisdom: Politikê Aretê and 'Logosophia'" *Philosophy & Rhetoric.* Vol. 39, No. 4, 2006

[20] Bakaoukas, Michael. "Gorgias the Sophist on Not-Being, A Wittgensteinian Interpretation." http://www.sorites.org/Issue_13/baka.htm.

[21] Bakaoukas, Michael. "Gorgias the Sophist on Not-Being, A Wittgensteinian Interpretation."

[22] Johnstone, Christopher Lyle. "Sophistical Wisdom: Politikê Aretê and 'Logosophia.'" *Philosophy & Rhetoric.* Vol. 39, No. 4, 2006

[23] Schiappa, Edward. "Interpreting Gorgias's 'Being' in 'On Not-Being or On Nature'." *Philosophy & Rhetoric.* Vol. 30, No.1, 1997.

[24] Bett, Richard. "Gorgias' Περὶ τοῦ μὴ ὄντος and its Relation to Skepticism." https://krieger.jhu.edu/philosophy/wp-content/uploads/sites/7/2013/02/Bett-Gorgiass-On-What-Is-Not.pdf.

[25] Schiappa, Edward. "Interpreting Gorgias's 'Being' in 'On Not-Being or On Nature'." *Philosophy & Rhetoric.* Vol. 30, No.1, 1997.

[26] McGilchrist lain. *The Master and His Emissary*. Yale University Press, 2009.

[27] Consigny, Scott. *Gorgias: Sophist and Artist*. University of South Carolina Press, 2001.

[28] Johnstone, Christopher Lyle. "Sophistical Wisdom: Politikê Aretê and 'Logosophia'" *Philosophy & Rhetoric.* Vol. 39, No. 4, 2006.

[29] Consigny, Scott. *Gorgias: Sophist and Artist*. University of South Carolina Press, 2001.

[30] Consigny, Scott. *Gorgias: Sophist and Artist.*

[31] Consigny, Scott. *Gorgias: Sophist and Artist.*

[32] Shakespeare, William. *Romeo and Juliet*. (New Folger's ed.), Washington Square Press/Pocket Books, 2004.

[33] Shakespeare, William. *Romeo and Juliet.*

[34] Shakespeare, William. *Henry IV Part One*. (New Folger's ed.), Washington Square Press/Pocket Books, 2020.

[35] Consigny, Scott. *Gorgias: Sophist and Artist*. University of South Carolina Press, 2001.

[36] Consigny, Scott. *Gorgias: Sophist and Artist.*

[37] Shakespeare, William. *Antony and Cleopatra.* (New Folger's ed.), Washington Square Press/Pocket Books, 2005.

[38] Magnusson, Lynne and David Shalkwyk (eds.) *The Cambridge Companion to Shakespeare's Language.* Cambridge University Press, 2019.

[39] Shakespeare, William. "Sonnet 90." *The Complete Sonnets and Poems*. Oxford University Press, 2002.

[40] Consigny, Scott. *Gorgias: Sophist and Artist*. University of South Carolina Press, 2001.

[41] Consigny, Scott. *Gorgias: Sophist and Artist.*

[42] Beckett, Samuel. *Waiting for Godot*. Faber and Faber, 1959.

[43] Consigny, Scott. *Gorgias: Sophist and Artist*. University of South Carolina Press, 2001.

[44] Shakespeare, William. *Titus Andronicus.* (New Folger's ed.), Washington Square Press/Pocket Books, 2020.

[45] Shakespeare, William. *Titus Andronicus.*

[46] Shakespeare, William. *Titus Andronicus.*

[47] Johnstone, Christopher Lyle. "Sophistical Wisdom: Politikê Aretê and 'Logosophia'" *Philosophy & Rhetoric.* Vol. 39, No. 4, 2006.

[48] Johnstone, Christopher Lyle. "Sophistical Wisdom: Politikê Aretê and 'Logosophia'."

[49] Johnstone, Christopher Lyle. "Sophistical Wisdom: Politikê Aretê and 'Logosophia'."

[50] Johnstone, Christopher Lyle. "Sophistical Wisdom: Politikê Aretê and 'Logosophia'."

[51] Shakespeare, William. "Venus and Adonis." *The Complete Sonnets and Poems*. Oxford University Press, 2002.

[52] Consigny, Scott. *Gorgias: Sophist and Artist*. University of South Carolina Press, 2001.

[53] Consigny, Scott. *Gorgias: Sophist and Artist*.

[54] Shakespeare, William. "Venus and Adonis." *The Complete Sonnets and Poems*. Oxford University Press, 2002.

[55] Shakespeare, William. "Venus and Adonis."

[56] Shakespeare, William. "Venus and Adonis."

[57] Johnstone, Christopher Lyle. "Sophistical Wisdom: Politikê Aretê and 'Logosophia'" *Philosophy & Rhetoric.* Vol. 39, No. 4, 2006.

Chapter Three: Camp

Gorgias demands the audience be 'fools,' but he is also demanding they view reality in 'quotation marks'; that is, with a fiercely critical eye. To this end, Gorgias' performances were what we might call meta-theatrical today: framed to remind viewers they were not truth. The four extant texts attributed to Gorgias are all monologues in which Gorgias plays a character or 'role.' In *On Nature or the Non-existent*, he plays a philosopher, in *Encomium of Hele*n, an orator, in *Defense of Palamedes*, a lawyer, and In *Epitaphios,* a eulogist. Consigny reminds us Gorgias' performances featured "exaggerated theatricality or 'acting,' wearing the traditional purple robes of the rhapsodes" (167).[1] In fact, Gorgias' presentations are not described as seeming to be completely in earnest. Consigny describes them as "frequently witty and occasionally bawdy, but rarely if ever moving" (166).[2] At the end of *Encomium of Helen*, Gorgias "characterizes his own work as paignon or 'amusement' ... suggesting that the text may not in some sense be serious" (6).[3]

Gorgias' performances were not just generally unserious, they were parodic. Consigny says: "Gorgias' texts mock themselves as well as other texts" (176).[4] Each of his texts was a parody of a certain style of speech, a certain rhetorical approach, from philosophical treatise to funeral oration, from impassioned plea to legal defence. And Gorgias "exaggerates the tropes of the genre in ways that render his text even more artificial than others in the genre" (172).[5] Gorgias' 'Epitaphios' is "an imitation of the orations delivered by Athenian citizens selected by the city itself" (172).[6] Gorgias' parodic style was announced by the choice of such unlikely subjects for his defences, as "by praising the reviled Helen of Troy, Gorgias in effect announces his work as parodic" (174).[7]

But Consigny's summary of Gorgias' style makes it clear that Gorgias' 'tongue in cheek' approach had a very serious intent:

> Gorgias' style may best be characterised as 'parodic' in that he adapts to the conventions of diverse discourses while playfully drawing attention to the conventions of those discourses and the rhetoricity of every text ... he foregrounds the conventions of the discourse in order to expose the strategies his foundationalist rivals use to deceive audiences into believing that their arguments or texts are objectively valid ... he deconstructs the assertions by self-effacing Eleatic philosophers who present themselves as speaking the voice of reason ... By displaying the rhetoricity of every text, he shows his audience that all arguments including his own are contingent, situated fabrications that are 'true' only insofar as they are endorsed by specific audiences. (30)[8]

Should this be the end of this exploration of the similarities between Gorgias and Shakespeare? For, surely, Shakespeare's tragedies were not 'parodic', but — in the classic sense of Greek tragedy — they purge us of pity and fear. To suggest anything else is deeply radical.

Keep in mind that, although Gorgias' style was 'parodic,' its serious intent required his speeches to have a hypnotic effect. His intention — to make the audiences aware of the falseness of all rhetoric — could only be achieved by completely swaying the audience to any particular point of view. In essence, if Gorgias had not been able to convince his audiences of what he was saying, then there would be no point to his rhetoric. If he was merely being silly, or if what he was saying could be too easily dismissed as false, then the audience would be distant from the work and uninvolved. In other words, hearing Gorgias speak would not be like watching a horror movie today. When we go to horror movies these days we are rarely frightened, but pretend that we are. Instead — think of a movie by Ingmar Bergman — or any other master director. When we leave the theatre, we shake our heads, trying to yank ourselves back to dull reality. To imagine that Gorgias was *merely* a comic writer, is to misinterpret him — for how could he show us the danger of being fooled if we were not completely taken in?

Surely Shakespeare's work was not parodic — even if sometimes it's difficult to figure out what he was saying, or to pin down his point of view. Audiences weep — and justly so — when Lear and his daughter are sentenced to jail, and yet Lear (in his madness?) seems to imagine they will live there 'happily ever after':

> Come, let's away to prison:
> We two alone will sing like birds i' the cage:
> When thou dost ask me blessing, I'll kneel down,
> And ask of thee forgiveness: so we'll live,
> And pray, and sing, and tell old tales, and laugh
> At gilded butterflies and hear poor rogues
> Talk of court news; and we'll talk with them too-
> Who loses and who wins; who's in, who's out-
> And take upon's the mystery of things,
> As if we were God's spies. (5.3.9-18)[9]

But what if *not* taking Shakespeare entirely seriously doesn't mean challenging the profundity of his work? What if not taking his work seriously makes it even more profound?

What if Shakespeare, like Gorgias — by inhabiting the style, the form, the particular language of each individual speaker with a kind of virtuoso accuracy — was fooling us — not just for the sake of fooling — but *to show us how profoundly we can be fooled*? Trevor McNeely says the message of Shakespeare's work lies not in the ideas any character expresses at any given moment; instead Shakespeare's entire oeuvre reminds us "that we can build a perfectly satisfactory reality on thin air and never think to question it" (121).[10]

It's important to remember that it is only relatively recently that Shakespeare's plays were taken seriously. This began when David Garrick and other 'bardolators' transformed him into an icon, 150 years after his death. During the Restoration, Shakespeare was considered a comic writer who had stumbled accidentally on the tragic form. Thomas Rymer viewed *Othello* as an inept tragedy: "There is in this Play, some burlesk, some humour, and ramble of Comical Wit, some shew, and some mimicry to divert the spectator: but the tragical part is, plainly none other, than a Bloody Farce, without salt or savour" (1).[11]

Samuel Johnson took it somewhat for granted that Shakespeare lacked a tragic sensibility, and (to quote Milton Crane),

> indulged his natural disposition, and his natural disposition as Rymer remarked, had led him to comedy. In tragedy he often writes with great appearance of toil and study, what is written at last with little felicity; but in his scenes, he produces without labour, what no labour can improve. In tragedy he is always struggling after some occasion to be comick; but in comedy he seems to repose or to luxuriate, as in a mode of thinking congenial to his nature ... His tragedy seems to be skill, his comedy to be instinct. (1)[12]

We might think that no critic today would ever think to characterize one of Shakespeare's tragedies as a comedy. Yet, modern day critics routinely challenge the genre of Shakespeare's less popular works. Plays like *Titus Andronicus, Richard II*, and *Antony and Cleopatra* make critics uncomfortable — as do poems like *Venus and Adonis* and *Shakespeare's Sonnets. Titus Andronicus* seems at times to be so unintentionally funny some find it difficult to believe Shakespeare was the author. And, others have claimed — due to the unsympathetic, unappealing nature of its tragic hero — that Richard II is actually not the leading character of the play named after him. These creations are often dismissed as aberrations, and treated with embarrassment. The accepted wisdom is that Shakespeare's tragedies must be approached with the utmost seriousness. If we happen to come upon a play or poem that teeters on the edge of its genre, then 'the bard' was just having a bad day.

Modern day critic Richard Lanham rejects *Venus and Adonis* for the same reason Restoration critics dismissed *Othello*:

> What does the narrator [i.e. Shakespeare] think of Venus and Adonis? He does not think at all. What do we think of him? He possesses rich poetic power but no judgment to go with it. To him, Shakespeare has leant his pen, not his mind. Such a divorce, perfect as it is for a satire of love and love's language, has caused serious misunderstanding. *Venus and Adonis* is a complex rhetorical structure to which sincerity supplies the wrong entry [...] The poem's comedy tempts us to deny it any seriousness whatever, to blunt its pathos, to render it a perfect trifle [...] Why include such pathos only to cancel it? (88-91)[13]

The same objections have been raised to *Titus Andronicus.* Alexander Leggatt says: "The extravagance of its action takes it to the edge of grotesque comedy" (249).[14] (It's interesting to note, too, that a play which we find so inscrutable today was apparently one of Shakespeare's most popular works during his lifetime.) A recent production of *Titus Andronicus* by the Royal Shakespeare Company took the bull by the horns, foregrounding our present day discomfort with the play's tone. According to Katherine Wooten it "delights in, rather than castigates, the farce and fun that can be had with a stage heaving with mutilated corpses, as spouts of blood whistle over the heads of unwitting members of the stalls."[15]

The Arden Shakespeare recounts 19th century Shakespeare critic A.C. Bradley's response to *Antony and Cleopatra.* He said it lacked "that consistently tragic high seriousness to which he responded in *Lear* and *Macbeth*, but [he] accepts the fact in this play Shakespeare attempted 'something different'" (48).[16] Cynthia Marshall sees that the leading characters of the play are viewed with a somewhat jaundiced eye: "Shakespeare scours received myths with skepticism" (305).[17]

Near the end of the play — in a moment of self-denigration — Cleopatra muses on the possibility that her legacy may be remembered only in an indecent performance by a drag queen: "I shall see / Some squeaking Cleopatra boy my greatness / I' th' posture of a whore" (5.2.266-68).[18] Why this mention of theatrical crossdressing at a moment when Shakespeare is attempting to elicit our sympathy for Cleopatra's plight? After all, in Shakespeare's day, Cleopatra would have been played by a boy. Is Shakespeare making a self-conscious joke about at the expense of our sympathy with her? Or is he — by acknowledging the possible obscenity and/or ridiculousness of a boy actor playing a full grown, fully sensuous, tragic woman — insuring that we will most assuredly *not* laugh?

The fact that Shakespeare chose mythical figures of dubious reputation as the heroes of his tragedies was a nod to Gorgias, who so famously offered his audiences a defence of Helen of Troy. The unlikely heroes of Shakespeare's tragedies were a signal to early modern audiences that the plays were meant to be viewed with something other than straight-faced reverence. Even his most celebrated tragic heroes often seem improper subjects for our unalloyed sympathy.

Aristotle defines tragedy as "an imitation in verse of characters of a higher type"[19] — in direct opposition to comedy, which is "an imitation of characters of a lower type — not, however, in the full sense of the word bad, the ludicrous being merely a subdivision of the ugly."[20] It would have been difficult for early modern audiences *not* to take Cleopatra for a whore — that is, a typical destroyer of men. And Antony — because he is so brutally emasculated by his love for her — would have been a difficult hero for early modern audiences to respect. David Bevington acknowledges that the play falls short of tragedy because the characters are not typical tragic heroes: "Self knowledge and tragic greatness emerge only belatedly and ambiguously. A dominant motif is the irreverent treatment of great historical figures" (68-69).[21]

Richard II is the character Shakespeare critics have voted least likely to succeed as tragic hero. Some insist that the moderate, eloquent, reasonable Bolingbroke is actually the main character. Yet, the play belongs to Richard and his profusely effuse, hyperbolic, self-indulgent, self-aggrandizing speechifying. He consistently overdramatizes everything to such an extent that the other characters remark on the inappropriateness of his responses to the trials that beset him. It's easy to see how — in what is most likely an early play — Shakespeare attempts to draw his tragedy directly from a comic vein. In other words, Richard's overblown, euphuistic, repetitive, alliterative, paradoxical, flamboyantly figurative speeches are both sad and funny at the same time.

In one monologue, Richard begins by employing a parody of Marlowe's famous praise of Helen of Troy to describe his own face, euphuistically and self-consciously implying a figure of speech called antanaclasis:

> Was this the face that faced so many follies,
> And was at last out-faced by Bolingbroke?
> A brittle glory shineth in this face:
> As brittle as the glory is the face ... (4.1. 296-99)[22]

Richard sets himself a rhetorical challenge, providing us with another of Shakespeare's ridiculously hyperbolic metaphors. His pain is so intense he could dig a grave with tears:

> Or shall we play the wantons with our woes,
> And make some pretty match with shedding tears?
> As thus, to drop them still upon one place,
> Till they have fretted us a pair of graves
> Within the earth; and, therein laid, — there lies
> Two kinsmen digg'd their graves with weeping eyes.
> Would not this ill do well? (3.3. 269-75)[23]

Bolingbroke finds this funny — as does Richard II himself. Much in the manner of Cleopatra (and so many other Shakespearean heroes), he acknowledges his own ridiculousness: "Well, well, I see / I talk but idly, and you laugh at me" (3.1.175-76).[24] Harry Berger mentions that some see Richard II "as a politically incompetent knave ... who is the butt of the play's irony" (239).[25] The play is not often produced on the modern stage for this very reason.

It's important to remember that *Richard II* was a popular, though controversial, play in Shakespeare's time. We know this because it was given an infamous performance — one that, in fact, might make us think twice about whether Shakespeare intended the play to be treated with reverence. On his return from Ireland in 1601, the Earl of Essex mounted an ill-fated 'rebellion' against the Queen. The night before the rebellion, there was a performance of *Richard II* by Shakespeare's acting company — The Lord Chamberlain's Men. The play concerns the deposition of a decadent and irresponsible king, and thus clearly had the potential to serve as an incitement to mob violence. An inquiry was made into why the Chamberlain's Men decided to perform that play on the eve of Essex's invasion. At the inquiry Auguste Philips — the spokesman for the Lord Chamberlain's Men — made this speech defending the players, stating that, in essence, they were tricked into producing a play, when they hadn't really wanted to perform it:

> Where this examinant and his friends were determined to have played some other play holding that play of King Richard to be so old and so long out of use as that they should have small or no company at it. But at their request this examinant and his friends were content to play it the Saturday and had their 40 shillings more than the ordinary for it and so played it accordingly.[26]

Philips seems to be saying that even though the play was somewhat of an 'ex-hit' at the time, the generous payment they received was persuasion enough to perform it.

What happened after that is really interesting. The Lord Chamberlain's Men were not held accountable for producing this possibly revolutionary play on the eve of an insurrection. More interesting still, Shakespeare was never asked to testify at the hearing. And finally — on the evening before Essex was beheaded for his part in the uprising, the Queen asked for a private performance of *Richard II*. She was fully conscious of the irony, as she is rumoured to have said: 'I am Richard II, know ye not that?' Even if Elizabeth did not actually say this (and it is disputed) — why would she request a private performance of a play which could easily be seen as an indictment of herself and her own rule, a play in which *she herself would* be identified with a decadent and effeminate king? Perhaps it was because she — like Richard II — had a sense of humour. If Edward de Vere was Shakespeare, this would explain why the playwright was never prosecuted — because both he and Elizabeth were fully aware that Shakespeare's tragedies, as moving as they were, could also be appreciated on another level — as perfectly calculated fooling.

And, it will not do at all to suggest that *Richard II* is atypical. In fact, the character seems like a trial run for Hamlet. Hamlet also has a tendency to denigrate himself, digress, and is markedly effeminate — not only in the artificiality of his language, and not merely because he is so reluctant to take up his sword. Indeed, Hamlet continuously reminds himself of his own ridiculousness, which he often relates to gender insecurity. He compares himself to a woman: "Am I a coward? Who calls me a villain? Breaks my pate across? Plucks off my beard and blows it in my face?" (2.2.598-600)[28] He later refers to his worries as "but foolery, but it is such a kind of gainsgiving as would perhaps trouble a woman" (5.2.229-30).[29] Hamlet even compares himself to a male prostitute: "Must I like a whore unpack my heart with words / And fall a-cursing like a very drab, a scullion!" (2.2. 614-16).[30] That Hamlet's extended grief over his father's death is absurdly effeminate is abundantly clear to Claudius: "But to persever / In obstinate condolement ... 'Tis unmanly grief" (1.2.96-98).[31]

Compare this to Laertes who — when he discovers the death of his beloved sister Ophelia — cries briefly, and then says of his tears: "When these are gone, / The woman will be out" (4.7.214-15).[32] Laertes knows how to mourn like a man, that is, to get it over with. At the end of *Hamlet*, the stage is littered with dead bodies. It's easy to be a little less moved than amused. (That's quite a lot of dead people!) In truth, we have mixed feelings about those so recently killed: the corpses include the murderer Claudius, his morally compromised queen Gertrude, and at least one useless effete courtier (Osric). It makes sense that this carnival of previously villainous cadavers is just a little ridiculous.

Hamlet is one of those dead bodies. We may not be unsympathetic, but our sympathy for him is strained — partially because it takes him a long time, quite often, simply to get to the point, and partially because we are never really sure exactly what his infamous 'problem' is. What is exactly the cause of his procrastination over avenging his father's death? He frames his angst in a manner that is existential enough, but also plays his madness like a game. 'To be or not to be,' is nearly always treated as serious psychological musing — but it's important to remember that it resembles all too closely the ontological jest that lies at the centre of *On Nature or the Non-Existent.*

T.S. Eliot was troubled not only by the vagueness of Hamlet's 'problem,' but also by its unsavoury associations. Though Eliot prefers not to identify Hamlet's personal issues directly, he clearly finds them inappropriate, "full of some stuff that the writer could not drag to light, contemplate, or manipulate into art" (58).[33] He asks if Hamlet, as a character, is the appropriate embodiment of tragedy. Is he someone who might, as Aristotle suggests, be the subject of our admiration? Does his death matter to the future of Denmark, or any other country? For that matter, does it matter to us? Or is he just a somewhat demented, obnoxious — although very thoughtful — nay, pithy, and very witty — young man?

Horatio, the only living member of the Danish court left on stage at the end of the play, eulogizes Hamlet as a 'sweet prince.' There *is* something sweet about him, even if it is simply his frankness about his lack of self esteem — and his tortured inability to stop going on about it. Arguably, it is impossible not to be charmed by him, impossible not to have *some* sympathy. But to suggest that Hamlet exists entirely outside the context of the ironic, paradoxical, artificial, and the absurd is, itself, ridiculous.

Is it possible to be both deeply moved by Shakespeare's plays and also to chuckle — *at precisely the same time*? If this were so, then Shakespeare's plays could be classified as camp. Camp is a form of gay humour that finds its origins in a reaction to homosexual oppression. It was first identified by Susan Sontag in her essay "Notes on Camp." Sontag identifies Lyly as one of the earliest purveyors of the style, and she comes very close to including Shakespeare as well: "A pocket history of Camp might, of course, begin farther back — with the mannerist artists like Pontormo, Rosso, and Caravaggio, or the extraordinarily theatrical painting of Georges de La Tour, or Euphuism (Lyly, etc.) in literature" (282).[34] She goes on to say, "*Titus Andronicus* and *Strange Interlude* are almost Camp, or could be played as Camp" (285),[35] and adds "why is the atmosphere of Shakespeare's comedies (*As You Like It*, etc.) not epicene [...] the relation to nature was quite different then" (281-82).[36] She goes on to suggest that the difference lies between an attempt to efface nature (camp) and a reverence for nature (not camp).

Here Sontag makes the common mistake of treating Shakespeare as a romantic poet. Shakespeare is not 'Wordsworthian' — he did not take his inspiration directly from the natural world. Though responsible for comparing his lover to a summer's day in *Shakespeare's Sonnets*, Shakespeare' relationship to beauty was much more complex than simply an adoration of trees and flowers. Grammar — one of the three early modern subjects of study in the 'classical trivium' — had a very different relationship to the natural world than science does today. Nature was, for the early modern grammarian, a book which could be read like a poem, and a poem was, in its own way, equivalent to nature. What the rhetorician thought of nature, and particularly the way he spoke about it, was to be discovered — not through observing the physical world, but from searching his own imagination: his rhetorical 'memory,' the palace in his head where his favourite images were stored.

Shakespeare poetry was conceived before modern science existed, before the elucidation and cataloguing of the animal, vegetable, and mineral world that we now understand to be 'reality.' His work is less a description of nature than a creation of it. David Haley claims that the word 'nature' did not mean the same thing in Shakespeare's time as it does today. In *Shakespeare's Courtly Mirror*, Haley suggests that, when Bertram comes to understand himself in *All's Well That Ends Well*, it is not through a discovery of who he is, but of who he imagines himself to be. Similarly, in *Venus and Adonis* and *The Rape of Lucrece*, Shakespeare consistently speaks of art that replaces reality. Haley says that when Hamlet references 'holding a mirror up to nature' — "The nature Hamlet means is not the physical realized world ... investigated by modern science or naturalistic novelists. Rather 'nature' refers to what becomes apparent only in the mirror. Nature has no discernible feature (shape) until the dramatic mirror creates it" (34).[37]

Yet Sontag refuses to classify Shakespeare's work as 'camp,' claiming it displays reverence for nature. But it clearly does not. She seems to think that Shakespeare did not view nature as artificial — when that is precisely how he described nature in so many of his plays and poems. Sontag was not a stupid woman. Instead she may have wanted to avoid labelling Shakespeare as 'camp' because of two dangerous implications of such a proclamation. The most significant implication is that to view his work as camp would diminish its importance. The second implication is, that since camp is a 'gay' thing, if Shakespeare's work was camp, that would make Shakespeare gay. The second implication can be dispensed with immediately. It is ludicrous. In the early modern period, there was certainly same sex desire (and of course same sex activity), but no sexual identity to compare with what we now label homosexuality. We will never know precisely what Shakespeare's sexuality was.

The much more palpable, threatening fear is this: by classifying Shakespeare's work as camp we will somehow diminish its profundity and its influence. But Sontag — who must be given credit for defining the term — believes that camp is essentially profound. She says so quite explicitly at the end of her essay:

> Camp taste is a kind of love, love for human nature. It relishes, rather than judges, the little triumphs and awkward intensities of "character." ... Camp taste identifies with what it is enjoying. People who share this sensibility are not laughing at the thing they label as "a camp," they're enjoying it. Camp is a *tender* feeling. (293)[38]

Here Sontag has defined Gorgias' aesthetic sensibility. What Gorgias does is take the seductiveness of language, its ability to hypnotize us with its honeyed sweetness, and turn it into an 'agon,' or game. The game is this — will we buy what he is selling? Will we be persuaded by the elegance of his turn of phrase, by his wit? Make no mistake about it, this game is a very serious one; and an excruciating paradox lies at the very centre. For Gorgias knows that when he offers us different poems, he is offering us a choice of different realities, and our lives will be forever changed by the reality we choose.

The Greek word 'agon' means an assembly of people, but it also means a kind of game. Consigny quotes Nietzsche's definition of agon: "to perceive all matters of the intellect, of life's seriousness, of necessities, even of danger, as play" (74).[39] Consigny says Gorgias sees "every use of language as occurring in an agon or game" (74).[40] For Gorgias, reality was not created through our observation of the world (as Aristotle and Plato suggested) because Gorgias believed reality is not discretely observable. Instead, what is real is defined by the artist *in collaboration with the audience*. For it is the audience who considers the realities an artist proposes, and decides whether or not to accept it.

In Greek culture, the sophists floated many different versions of truth in the marketplace. It was part of a game — or agon — in which audiences decided on — literally voted on — which rhetor was speaking the truth. Essentially, it is the job of the sophist to bring competing notions of reality into the public square, and let the public come to an agreement on what reality actually is. Reality is contingent on eloquence — on poetry — and the audience knows it. They also know that their notion of reality may change if another poet comes along and convinces them of something else. As Consigny says: "Every account is always a partial and partisan assertion by a rhetor engaged in specific agon. In some cases clever rhetors are able to conceal their own situatedness ... they effectively efface themselves before what appears to be an objective truth" (92).[41] We must not "forget that there will always be alternative ways of construing the situation" (92).[42]

We must approach each of the characters in Shakespeare's plays and poems as a sophist. Shakespeare was a remarkable craftsman who was able to gift each character with a very personal and particular manner of speaking — their own metre, quirks, fondness for poetry or prose, indulgence in complex metaphors — or tendency towards simple (or even obscene) ejaculation. When Shakespeare's characters speak, they are — like Gorgias — offering different theories of what reality is. They are offering a variety of solutions to a variety of existential quandaries. It is not a matter of whether Shylock or Iago is right or wrong, or good or bad. The sophistical question is — have they convinced you of their truth? Coleridge's characterization of Iago as the 'motive hunting of motiveless malignity' is particularly relevant here. Each of Shakespeare's characters is a version of Iago — as Iago is perhaps the most potent example of a liar and a sophist — one who we find ourselves detesting, but at the same time, despite ourselves, enjoying — or even liking.

Shakespeare's plays are certainly founded in skepticism — but sophism is the key to our understanding of them. The self-conscious artifice that is accentuated by attenuated and artificial language, by invented words, by relentless paradox, unlikely metaphors, and the highly imperfect characters who sometimes impugn their own motives — this is part of Shakespeare's particular 'camp' strategy to consistently remind us not only that what we are seeing is not 'real,' but that it could, in fact, be a troubling or dangerous mystification.

What is so astounding about Shakespeare's achievement is that it is in direct contrast to the Church-sanctioned religious theatre which preceded it. Modern western drama was barely kept alive during the medieval period. When it did surface, it was personified by mystery plays: stories from the Bible performed in front of a church or on wagons. The purpose of these plays was to preach, through the use of pontificating allegories — as in *Everyman*. The early modern plays which preceded Shakespeare's were either comedies that skewered vice (*Ralph Roister Doister*) or ponderous tragedies that pointed audiences to virtue (*Gorboduc*). What all this rhetoric shared was a commitment to didacticism; their existence was justified through their Christian — or at the very least, educational — import. Theatre in early modern England was constantly under attack from the puritans. Even Shakespeare's contemporary, Sydney, had to justify all rhetoric (in *A Defence of Poetry*) — as the most effective mode of learning: "Who will be taught, if he be not moved with desire to be taught?" (22).[43]

Shakespeare's work never recommends virtue, it never tells us what is right or what is wrong, it does not preach a Christian ethic. Instead, it offers us choices that might empower us to choose our own reality. How did Shakespeare become Shakespeare? How did he develop his own personal — not so much a *moral* sensibility — but his *amoral* one? Shakespeare's sensibility was not only different in mood tone and intention to the sensibility of the medieval period; he wrote in direct opposition to it. He meant to destroy didacticism.

Endnotes

1 Consigny, Scott. *Gorgias: Sophist and Artist*. University of South Carolina Press, 2001.

2 Consigny, Scott. *Gorgias: Sophist and Artist*.

[3] Consigny, Scott. *Gorgias: Sophist and Artist.*

[4] Consigny, Scott. *Gorgias: Sophist and Artist.*

[5] Consigny, Scott. *Gorgias: Sophist and Artist.*

[6] Consigny, Scott. *Gorgias: Sophist and Artist.*

[7] Consigny, Scott. *Gorgias: Sophist and Artist.*

[8] Consigny, Scott. *Gorgias: Sophist and Artist.*

[9] Shakespeare. William. *King Lear*. Simon and Schuster Annotated edition, 2004.

[10] McNeely, Trevor. *Proteus Unmasked*. Lehigh University Press, 2004.

[11] Parker, G.F. "False Disproportion: Rymer on Othello." *The Cambridge Quarterly* Vol. 17, No. 1, Oxford University Press, 1988.

[12] Crane, Milton. "Shakespeare's Comedies and the Critics" *Shakespeare Quarterly*, Vol.15 No. 2, 1964, Oxford University Press.

[13] Lanham, Richard. "On the Narrator's Detachment." *Shakespeare's Sonnets and Poems* (Harold Bloom, ed.) Chelsea House, 1999.

[14] Leggat, Alexander. "Titus Andronicus: A Modern Perspective." *Titus Andronicus*, Simon and Schuster Annotated edition, 2005.

[15] Wooton, Katherine. "Titus Andronicus, Royal Shakespeare Company." *Aesthetica* (https://aestheticamagazine.com/titus-andronicus-royal-shakespeare-company/). October 8, 2013.

[16] Wilders, John. "Introduction." *Antony and Cleopatra*. Routledge, 1995.

[17] Marshall, Cynthia. "Antony and Cleopatra: A Modern Perspective" *Antony and Cleopatra.* (New Folger's ed.), Washington Square Press/Pocket Books, 1999.

[18] Shakespeare, William. *Antony and Cleopatra.* (New Folger's ed.), Washington Square Press/Pocket Books, 1999.

[19] Aristotle. *Poetics*. The Internet Classic's Archive, 1994. http://classics.mit.edu/Aristotle/poetics.1.1.html.

[20] Aristotle. *Poetics*.

[21] Bevington, David. "Introduction." *Antony and Cleopatra.* Cambridge University Press, 2005.

[22] Shakespeare, William *Richard II*. (New Folger's ed.), Washington Square Press/Pocket Books, 1996.

[23] Shakespeare, William *Richard II*.

[24] Shakespeare, William *Richard II*.

[25] Berger Jr., Harry. 'Richard II: A Modern Perspective.' *Richard II*. Simon and Schuster Annotated edition, 1996.

[26] Morris, Sylvia. "Shakespeare's Richard II and the Essex rebellion." *The Shakespeare Blog*. http://theshakespeareblog.com/2014/02/shakespeares-richard-ii-and-the-essex-rebellion/

[27] Shakespeare, William. *Hamlet.* (New Folger's ed.), Washington Square Press/Pocket Books, 2012.

[28] Shakespeare, William. *Hamlet.*

[29] Shakespeare, William. *Hamlet.*

[30] Shakespeare, William. *Hamlet.*

[31] Shakespeare, William. *Hamlet.*

[32] Shakespeare, William. *Hamlet.*

[33] Eliot, T.S. *The Sacred Wood and Early Major Essays*. Dover Publications, 1998.

[34] Sontag, Susan. *Against Interpretation*. Dell, 1966.

[35] Sontag, Susan. *Against Interpretation*.

[36] Sontag, Susan. *Against Interpretation*.

[37] Hayley, David. *Shakespeare's Courtly Mirror: Reflexivity and Prudence in* All's Well That Ends Well. University of Delaware Press, 1993.

[38] Sontag, Susan. *Against Interpretation*. Dell, 1966.

[39] Consigny, Scott. *Gorgias: Sophist and Artist*. University of South Carolina Press, 2001.

[40] Consigny, Scott. *Gorgias: Sophist and Artist.*

[41] Consigny, Scott. *Gorgias: Sophist and Artist.*

[42] Consigny, Scott. *Gorgias: Sophist and Artist.*

[43] Sydney, Philip. *The Defence of Poesy*. Cambridge University, 1898.

Chapter Four: Didacticism

Shakespeare is responsible for his plays. That he meant us to treat his work as bewitching deception, magic (or perhaps even as 'camp') does not let him off the hook. Modern scholars nurture a studied ignorance of Shakespeare's background in the classics, as such deep learning would have been impossible for the 'man from Stratford.' This has resulted in a blithe obliviousness to Shakespeare's obvious skeptical intentions. But make no mistake; Shakespeare's skepticism is not merely an accidental side-effect of his prodigious classical learning. It was his *intention* that we be troubled by the lack of moral guidance in his plays. Shakespeare himself engineered our confusion and anger deliberately (and perhaps, even perversely). It was a direct result of his antagonism towards the culture of Christian didacticism that preceded him.

Shakespeare's plays are steeped in medieval chivalric notions, and medieval texts are Christian *moral* texts. Mark Rose says: "Not just Othello's imagination but, I would suggest, Shakespeare's own, is informed by the patterns of chivalric romance" (295).[1] The first books printed in England by William Caxton (1476) were lessons in the form of medieval chivalric allegories — *The Book of Order and Chivalry* by Raymon Llull, and Malory's *Le Morte d'Arthur*. Queen Elizabeth herself kept chivalry alive because, after the British conversion to Protestantism, the public yearned for their old Catholic holidays. Yates says the Accession Day Tilts — Queen Elizabeth's royal event involving chivalric competitions and rituals performed for the queen — “bridged religious gaps” (110).[2] Shakespeare’s debt to Castiglione’s *The Book of the Courtier* has been acknowledged by scholars, and Edward de Vere (who was a star performer in the Queen’s tilts) wrote an introduction to it, acknowledging his reverence for the medieval nobleman/ warrior (an image modified in the 1500s by the addition of the ideal courtier’s poetic bent). Mark Anderson gives us this excerpt from de Vere's introduction to *The Book of the Courtier* where de Vere employs the skeptical, Shakespearean notion of art surpassing nature to praise the medieval paradigm:

> For what more difficult, more noble, or more magnificent task has anyone ever undertaken than our author Castiglione, who has drawn for us the figure and model of a courtier, a work to which nothing can be added, in which there is no redundant word, a portrait which we shall recognize as that of the highest and most perfect type of man. And so, although nature herself has made nothing perfect in every detail, yet the manners of men exceed in dignity that with which nature has endowed them; and he who surpasses others has here surpassed himself, and has even out done nature which by no one has ever been surpassed. (52)[3]

But Shakespeare’s relationship to his cultural antecedents was not untroubled. Lewis tells us that in *The Anxiety of Influence*, Harold Bloom writes of “the ephebe poet’s necessary early imitation of the precursor” (128).[4] Bloom theorizes that, first, a young author deals with his direct literary antecedents by imitating them. Later, the poet invents “strong misreadings of the precursor which involve mitigating (in phantasy) the castrating influence” (I.130).[5] Bloom considers Marlowe to be Shakespeare’s most formidable literary antecedent. But Lewis reminds us there are many possible candidates. Chaucer,

Gower, and the medieval morality plays were Shakespeare's most significant precursors. It's no accident that Chaucer's *Canterbury Tales* provides the source material for two of Shakespeare's plays (*Troilus and Cressida* and *The Two Noble Kinsmen*), or that John Gower (the narrator of *Pericles*) was a medieval poet and a contemporary of Chaucer.

Shakespeare would have known of the medieval passion plays originally performed on the steps of churches — later on wagons — based on Bible stories. He would have also been familiar with morality plays like *Everyman* that feature characters representing specific vices or virtues. Thomas Fulton writes: "Many scholars have explored Shakespeare's relationship with the drama of the late Middle Ages, showing that Shakespearean playgoers would have been sensitive to homiletic modes of expression from this still-active form of representation" (126-27).[6] Frederik Tupper affirms that Christian moralizing similar to the passion plays is found in both Chaucer and Gower: "To maintain that the poet had in these tales no intention of illustrating the Vices ... necessitates not only a disregard of all evidence but an insensibility to the trend of medieval thought" (105).[7]

In *Pericles*, Shakespeare displays his deep ambivalence toward the literary tradition that preceded him. It is a particularly strange play, usually assumed to have been written in 1608 because it is listed in the Stationer's Register for that year. Ben Jonson, in his "Ode to Himself" (1629), refers to *Pericles* as "some mouldy tale ... stale as the shrieve's crusts."[8] Indeed, the fantastical plot resonates with incidents from Edward de Vere's youth — particularly those that occurred between 1575 and 1576, when, at age 25, he toured France, Germany, and Italy. De Vere was deeply troubled by the suspicion that the daughter conceived by his wife Ann Cecil was illegitimate. *Pericles* not only features a well-travelled hero, but could very well have been a hopeful imagining of the loving reunion with his wife and daughter that de Vere longed for on his return from Italy, but alas, never had.

However, it is the play's strained relationship with didacticism that marks *Pericles* as an early work. The play is narrated by medieval poet John Gower, who appears before each act. David Hoeniger observes that "with his quaint archaic, moralizing lines ... there is no parallel for such a character or such an effect anywhere else in Shakespeare" (463).[9] Gower not only fills us in on the background plot but points us towards a lesson. Critics have struggled to understand this odd character. Many suggest he's inserted as comic relief. The problem is, he's just not that funny. Gower appears in *Pericles* for one reason only — to signal young Shakespeare's discomfort with Christian moralizing. Shakespeare's fundamental instincts — as well as his readings of Greek skepticism and Gorgias — would have prompted him to abandon didacticism. But a play without a moral would run directly counter to the sometimes puritan spirit of the times — exemplified by Philip Sydney, who, in *The Defence of Poesy*, defends poets as exemplary moralists.

So Gower gives the audience what medieval spectators would have expected, but with a caveat. The narrator moralizes, but Shakespeare is clearly making fun of him as old-fashioned. Gower is like a comic, charming, yet curmudgeonly uncle; a bungling relic from another era. Gower also sometimes speaks in Latin — the medieval language of poetry. Hoeniger describes the "stiff tetrameter style" and "Archaic rhymes" (464)[10] that distinguish Gower as an echo from the past. Hoeniger also notes that Gower articulates his concern over whether a *modern* audience will like his story: "[H]e expresses hope that it still may be found acceptable to his new listeners 'born in these later times, / When wit's more ripe'" (463).[11]

The play opens with Pericles discovering an incestuous relationship between Antiochus and his daughter. Gower wags his finger at them: "Bad child; worse father! To entice his own / To evil should be done by none" (1.1.27-28).[12] He returns at the end to remind us which of the characters are good and which are not: "In Antiochus you have heard / Of monstrous lust the true and just reward" (Epilogue.1-2)[13] whereas, Helicanus is a "figure of truth, of faith, of loyalty" (Epilogue.8).[14] You would be right to think — not only that a judgemental narrator is *a*typical of Shakespeare — but that such moralizing rests in opposition to his very sensibility.

Gower's preachy monologues are juxtaposed against the improbable, even shocking, incidents that constitute the play's plot, ranging from dastardly deeds to noble heroism and peppered with sheer magic. The unlikely events in the play, as well as the evil deeds committed by some of the characters, imply a pagan context. Pericles is directed by the Goddess Diana to seek out his wife at Diana's temple. When he discovers his wife, he cries out: "This, this no more you Gods! Your present kindness / Makes my past miseries seem like sport" (5.3.47-48).[15] If Gower's homiletic intrusions were excluded, the characters would seem like blameless pawns of the pagan gods.

Pericles also features a fascinating encounter between Marina and 'two gentlemen.' Marina is Pericles' chaste young daughter. She has been sold into prostitution, but elects to steer potential clients away from having sex with her. In what is essentially a comic scene, Shakespeare displays his ambivalent attitude to the effects of Christian preaching. Marina is a chivalric damsel in distress and a paragon of Christian purity. It is not so much that Shakespeare makes fun of Marina as that he wishes to remind us that she is a character in a poem. Her defence against possible paramours is a simple, but unlikely, one: she lectures them on chastity.

Amazingly, it works. Or does it? Take a look at the dialogue the two Gentlemen. have after their visit:

> FIRST GENTLEMAN. Did you ever hear the like?
> SECOND GENTLEMAN. No, nor never shall do in such a place as this, she being once gone.
> FIRST GENTLEMAN. But to have divinity preached there! Did you ever dream of such a thing?
> SECOND GENTLEMAN. No, no. Come, I am for no more bawdy-houses. Shall's go hear the vestals sing? (4.5.1-7)[16]

Shakespeare did not mean for us to take this seriously. The Shakespeare we know would not be naive enough to think that two men a) might be so easily talked out of 'vice'; and b) after such a lecture, would promptly make their way to church. Or could Shakespeare be making a point, reminding us that, although Marina's virtue appears to be antique and of a 'fairy tale' variety, it is necessary for us to suspend our disbelief and trust it? Through the two Gentlemen, Shakespeare, by admitting his own self-consciousness about the precious anachronistic ridiculousness of the characters and situations he creates, grants us permission to believe in them.

The Taming of the Shrew is another early work by Shakespeare shaped by his struggle with didacticism. The play features an odd 'induction' (the Elizabethan term for 'introduction'). Taking a step beyond *Pericles*, this induction encourages us to view the play as an entertaining, fantastical alternate reality rather than as a moral lesson. Shakespeare's enduring comedy is traditionally viewed as a sexist, misogynist lecture enforcing the oppression of women. In fact, it is quite the opposite; though it teases us with the *expectation* of a moral lesson, instead, it supplies only theatrical magic — neatly replacing didactic poetry with pure metaphor.

The central character in *The Taming of The Shrew*, Petruchio, seeks to 'train' his wife, Katherine, in virtue. This 'virtue' consists primarily of submission to his every whim. It's tough to argue that *The Taming of the Shrew* is not a misogynistic play because Katherine is dragged about and denied both food and sleep to cure her of her 'shrewishness.' And, this shrewishness seems only to mean what we might today see as independence. Her final speech reeks of Stockholm syndrome: "Thy husband is thy lord, thy life thy keeper, / Thy head, thy sovereign" (5.2 152-3).[17] Kate even recommends to Hortensio's wife, "place your hand below your husband's foot / In token of which duty, if he please / My hand is ready, may it do him ease" (5.2 184-5).[18]

Do not be fooled: though 'shrew taming' may be the subject matter of the play, it is not its theme. For one thing, the notion that women needed to be controlled was not particularly Shakespearean; it was ubiquitous in early modern England. Men took a defensive position against both female sexuality and women themselves. (They were so afraid of female sexuality that women's bodies were banned from the stage). And the figure of the 'shrewish wife' (the nagging scold) — far from being unique to Shakespeare — embodied the fear of women's independence in many medieval and Renaissance plays. (Noah's wife — arguably the most entertaining character in the medieval mystery play *Noah's Flood* — is so dead set against the ark that she slaps her husband in the face.) Being a shrew was more than just a social inconvenience, it was deemed a misdemeanor under the law. The introduction to the Arden 'Shrew' tells us that "by the early seventeenth century cucking — binding a female offender to a stool and dunking her in water — had become a typical shaming ritual and may have been responsible for establishing 'scold' as a legal category adjudicated by secular courts" (46).[19] Of course, the fact that the 'shrew' was a common concept in Elizabethan culture — and ubiquitous in Elizabethan plays — doesn't lessen, for many, Kate's horrific surrender. But the play's induction is proof that Shakespeare's intention was *not* to preach.

The Taming of the Shrew is not the only Elizabethan play to feature an induction: Robert Y. Turner lists twelve other plays written between 1566 and 1599 that have them. Most of these plays feature what Turner calls 'causal inductions.' Early modern causal inductions removed the spectator from illusion, from the 'suspension of disbelief,' offering the audience not only dramatic context, but a moral one. The moral aspect of these causal inductions gave audiences a way to process plays that were less obviously preachy than the medieval ones they were so familiar with. Turner says:

> In short, it seems as if playwrights or audiences, conditioned by the habit of the moralities, could not rest assured that the characters' thoughts without an external correlative were dramatically sufficient to motivate action. Therefore, an additional allegorical exposition prefaced a concrete or literal story. (187)[20]

In contrast, the induction before *The Taming of the Shrew* is one of the few Turner labels a 'dream' induction. As in *Pericles*, Shakespeare is struggling with the issue of moralizing, but in *The Taming of the Shrew*, he comes down unequivocally against art as lesson.

In the two scene induction to *The Taming of* the *Shrew*, a drunken beggar named Sly is shoved onstage by the mistress of a pub; he consequently falls asleep. A Lord and his Huntsman play a trick on Sly, convincing him that he is a nobleman who has been slumbering for fifteen years. They provide Sly with the finest wine and food, a lovely well-spoken wife (played by a boy), and a play to view — in which a shrew is tamed. The first scene of this induction is the hatching of this plot, and in the second scene, Sly is convinced of his new identity.

Importantly, there is another version of *The Taming of the Shrew* — called *The Taming of a Shrew* — which features not only the induction found in *The Taming of the Shrew*, but several other, later appearances by the induction characters, who return at the end of the play to wrap things up. *The Taming of* a *Shrew* (almost only half the length of its sister text) is undoubtedly the inferior play. Scholars agree that it is either an earlier version of the play we know so well, or a 'bad quarto.' What's interesting is that the purpose of all of Sly's scenes in both versions of 'Shrew' is to convince us that the play about the shrewish wife that we are about to see is not so much a 'play' as another reality.

When the Lord first explains his plot to trick Sly, he suggests they furnish the room nicely, for "would not the beggar then forget himself?" (Induction.1.40).[21] This is the first clue that Sly is undergoing a magical, imaginative transformation. The Huntsman is concerned that "it would seem strange onto him [Sly] when he waked" (Induction.1.42).[22] The Lord agrees: "Even as a faltering dream or worthless jest" (Induction.1.43).[23] What they are providing for Sly is a dream — another reality — in competition with the one in which Sly actually lives. One of the strategies is to convince Sly that he was mad — or dreaming — when he lived his life as a beggar: "Persuade him that he hath been a lunatic, / And when he says he is, say that he dreams" (Induction 1. 62-63).[24]

Sly is being inducted into the club that Theseus describes in *A Midsummer Night's Dream*: 'The lunatic, the lover and the poet / Are of imagination compact" (5.1.7-8).[25] When Sly awakens, he is persuaded of his new identity — "I smell sweet savours and I feel soft things. / Upon my life, I am a Lord indeed" (Induction. 2.69-70).[26] He is told that a play is recommended for him by his doctor: "They thought it good you hear a play / And frame your mind to mirth and merriment / Which bars a thousand harms and lengthens life" (Induction. 2.131-33).[27] The play is 'cathartic' — it will make Sly happy, by releasing him from pain. It makes sense that Sly — raised on morality plays like Shakespeare's audience — might assume that what he was about to see was not really a play, but simply a diversion:

> SLY. A Christmas gambol or a tumbling ticket?
> SERVANT. No, my good Lord, it is more pleasing stuff.
> SLY. What, household stuff?
> SERVANT. It is a kind of history. (Induction 2.133-37)[28]

So Sly — much like the audience — must be instructed as to how to appreciate a play that offers no moral instruction.

As he settles in, Sly says: "And let the world slip: we shall ne'er be younger" (Induction. 2.139).[29] Sly is so hypnotized by the magic of the performance that he comes to believe that it is another reality — his world does slip away, and another takes its place. This point is emphasized in two additional scenes which only appear in *The Taming of a Shrew*. Wentersdorf mentions a moment in which Sly — like a child who is unfamiliar with suspension of disbelief — seems to mistake the characters for real people:

> SLIE. Sim, must they be married now?
> LORD. Aye, my Lord. (208)[30]

And when Tranio calls for a policeman, reality and fantasy have completely merged for Sly: he must be talked out of halting the stage action; he must be reminded he is watching a play. 'This is what the experience of a *real play* is like,' Shakespeare seems to be saying — 'What you are seeing is not simply a Christian moral lesson — be aware — you might imagine it's real':

> SLIE. I say weele haue no sending to prison.
> LORD. My Lord, this is but the play, they're but in jest. (208)[31]

The Taming of a Shrew features a brief epilogue, in which (according to Richard Hosley) Sly "informs the Tapster he has had a rare dream of how to tame a shrew, and sets off for home where, if necessary, he will apply the lesson he has learned from the comedy and tame his own wife" (19).[32] This suggests Shakespeare thinks the audience should take home a similar moral. But remember, Sly's promise is made after a drunken night in which he has been kicked out of the bar (by a woman no less) and 'deceived' into believing he is a great Lord. It is difficult to take his moral resolve seriously. Like the two gentlemen who promise to abandon lust for church after meeting Marina in *Pericles,* we are not meant to have faith in Sly's moral resolve. Instead, this final scene ironically accentuates the hopelessness of searching for moral redemption in a theatre of rhetoric. In *The Taming of the Shrew* (undoubtedly a later improvement on *The Taming of a Shrew*), Shakespeare removed all later appearances by Sly. Sly's own self disappears: he — like the theatre audience — becomes the hypnotized auditor of another reality.

Both the induction — and the central plot of *The Taming of the Shrew* — set themselves directly against didacticism. An acknowledged source for *The Taming of the Shrew* is *The Supposes* (1566, by George Gascoigne), an adaptation of Ariosto's *I Suppositi*. The situations in Gascoigne's play are very similar to those in *The Taming of the Shrew.* There is a servant who trades places with a master, and an appearance by a 'fake father' who is exposed by the appearance of the real father. But Seronsy suggests that Shakespeare was not just interested in stealing comic situations from *The Supposes.* For Elizabethan jargon, to 'suppose' meant to not only to disguise oneself:

> There is no reason to assume that the word "supposes" itself must be limited now or in sixteenth-century usage to mean only "substitutions" of characters for one another in a mere mechanical routine of outward disguise. For Elizabethans it had substantially the same values in meaning as it has for us: "supposition", "expectation", "to believe", "to imagine", "to guess", "to assume". If we keep before us this wider sense of the word, it is not difficult to see how it becomes a guiding principle of Petruchio's strategy in winning and taming the shrew. (15-16)[33]

Seronsy theorizes Petruchio's taming of Katherine is a radical aesthetic mentorship. Early on, Petruchio sees that Katherine has potential to be other than she appears. "The distinction is one between outer circumstance and inner conviction, a kind of triumph of personality over a world of stubborn outward 'fact' not quite so real as had been supposed" (20).[34] This notion matches Shakespeare's obsession with the paradox when the 'outside' of a person does not match the 'inside.' What makes Petruchio such a radical teacher, according to Seronsy, is that he believes there is a greater truth inside Katherine than the way she generally acts. Petruchio thinks that by 'supposing' — i.e. lying, he will be able to reveal Katherine's true self.

Petruchio wishes to contradict Katherine's 'reality' and replace it with another through suggestion (supposing).

Alone, he muses, "Say that she rail; why then I'll tell her plain / She sings as sweetly as a nightingale; / Say that she frown; I'll say she looks as clear / As morning roses newly wash'd with dew" (2.1. 169-72).[35] It gradually becomes clear that he will be acquainting Katherine with poetry — as it is poets who create reality through their imaginings. As Seronsy says: "Petruchio's is a triumph of the imagination" (24).[36] The process he goes through begins with replacing Katherine's outer appearance with what he imagines to be her inner essence. As they verbally spar, he tells her,

> No, not a whit; I find you passing gentle.
> T'was told me you were rough and coy and sullen,
> And now I find report a very liar,
> For thou are pleasant, gamesome, passing courteous,
> But slow in speech, yet sweet as springtime flowers.
> (2.1. 244-48)[37]

Petruchio persistently challenges the world of outward appearances, asking Katherine to come to terms with what he considers to be the inner essence of things. When he shows up dressed in 'motley,' he presents himself as a silly clown on the outside, yet asks Katherine to see beyond this to the thoughtful man beneath. After refusing to let her have the beautiful gown made expressly for her, he makes the point of his exercise clear:

> For 'tis the mind that makes the body rich
> And as the sun breaks through the darkest clouds,
> So honour peereth in the meanest habit.
> What is the jay more precious than the lark
> Because his feathers are more beautiful?" (4.3. 171-75.[38]

Gradually what seems at first to be merely the manipulation of Katherine's behaviour becomes epistemological theory. Petruchio's particular way of looking at the world is to recreate it in his own image. He has moved beyond simply helping Katherine imagine she is someone she appears not to be. By the end of the play, Petruchio emphatically insists that Katherine ignore the evidence of her senses. She must no longer see with her eyes, but instead — like the poet — with her soul. Petruchio is teaching Katherine how to lie: how to create another reality through 'supposing.' Once he has convinced her that the sun is what *he* says it is, she has entered a universe where a lie is more persuasive than truth. She agrees with him, saying,

> Then God be blest, it is the blessed sun,
> But sun it is not, when you say it is not
> And the moon changes even as your mind.
> What you have it named even that it is
> And so it shall be so for Katherine. (4.5.19-23)[39]

If we examine Katherine's final 'surrender' in this light, we see it does not so much offer proof that she is submitting to her husband than that she has become a master rhetor. The key here is Kate's sudden, felicitous discovery of her own eloquence; she learns nothing more useful than how to be a skillful liar. In her final speech she displays a kind of virtuoso rhetorical chicanery — Gorgian in style, and typical of an Elizabethan poet. What she has obviously gained from Petruchio's lessons is not submission, but the opposite — namely, the ability to persuade anyone of anything, and to create reality through poetry.

It is only at the end of the play that Katherine speaks at length, utilizing balanced nuances that echo Lyly's euphuism (i.e. *paromoion* — similar sounds either at the beginning or the end of words — and also, of course, *paradox*). In the first two lines, she offers a typical Shakespearean repetition — the 'un' prefix. To the Widow, she says: "Fie, fie, unknit that threatening and unkind brow" (5.2.142).[40] By the fourth line, she begins to sound very much like Shakespeare in the sonnets: "It blots thy beauty as frosts do bite the meads, / Confounds thy fame as whirlwinds shake fair bud" (5.2.145-46).[41] She has learned to be a skilled rhetor. So although the content of her final speech is 'anti-feminist,' it's important to remember that the ideas expressed by characters in Shakespeare's plays are often offensive to us. Ultimately it doesn't matter whether we agree with them or not — as Shakespeare is not taking sides with one idea or another, but simply making us aware of the power of persuasion.

It is ridiculous to suggest that in *The Taming of the Shrew* Shakespeare wishes to oppress women. In doing so, we must ignore the strong, proud, brilliant, sublimely persuasive females who are celebrated in a proto-feminist manner in so many of his other poems and plays — most of whom speak as eloquently as Kate at the end of *The Taming of the Shrew.* Must we abandon Viola, Rosalind, Venus, Cleopatra? What about Lucrece? The idea that language has enormous power to create reality is a theme that Shakespeare returns to again and again. If there is any 'theme' of *The Taming of the Shrew, that* is it. On the other hand, the idea that 'a woman must obey her husband' is not the theme of any other Shakespeare play — and is passionately contradicted by the actions of the women in *The Merry Wives of Windsor*. To say that *The Taming of the Shrew* is an anti-feminist play makes as about much sense as saying *Macbeth* is an anti-murder play or *Hamlet* was written to cure mankind of prevarication. It is incumbent on us to stop missing the forest for the trees! Shakespeare wishes to involve us in the attitudes of many of the characters simultaneously, and he refuses to select a favourite.

Early modern theatregoers would have been unsettled by this. It is quite possible that the amorality of Shakespeare's work made it a guilty pleasure for Elizabethans. This may have been one of the reasons it took so long for Ben Jonson to turn out the complete collection of Shakespeare's works. Though Jonson praises Shakespeare in his introduction to the first folio, Bate points out that, in his play *The Poetaster,* Jonson satirizes Shakespeare (and Marlowe) in the character of the Roman poet Ovid. Bate says it's clear in *The Poetaster* that Jonson disapproved of Ovid's work, calling it distinctly problematic, for there is little learning in him "concerning either 'virtues, manners, or policy.' His *Amores* contain nothing 'but incitation to lechery' and time spent reading him would be better employed on such authors that do minister both eloquence, and civil policy, and exhortation to virtue" (169).[42]

Bate observes that "there is a strong case for reading the character [of Ovid] as Jonson's composite of Marlowe and Shakespeare" (170).[43] For Elizabethans, Shakespeare *was* the Roman poet Ovid. And Ovid meant not only sexual license, but a committed opposition to didacticism.

Endnotes

1 Rose, Mark. "Othello's Occupation; Shakespeare and the Romance of Chivalry." *English Literary Renaissance.* Vol 15. No. 3.

2 Yates, Francis A. *Astraea: The Imperial Theme in the Sixteenth Century.* Routledge and Kegan Paul, 1975.

3 Anderson, Mark. "*Shakespeare by Another Name.*" Gotham, 2006.

4 Lewis, Alan D. "Shakespearean Seductions, or What's with Harold Bloom as Falstaff?" *Texas Studies in Literature and Language.* Vol 49 Number 7, University of Texas Press, 2007.

[5] Lewis, Alan D. "Shakespearean Seductions, or What's with Harold Bloom as Falstaff?" *Texas Studies in Literature and Language.*

[6] Fulton, Thomas. "Shakespeare's Everyman Measure for Measure and English Fundamentalism." *Journal of Medieval and Early Modern Studies.* Duke University Press, 2010.

[7] Tupper, Frederick. "Chaucer and the Seven Deadly Sins." *PMLA.* Vol. 29, No. 1 Cambridge University Press, 1914.

[8] Jonson, Ben. "Ode to Himself ['Come leave the loathéd stage']" *Poetry Foundation.* https://www.poetryfoundation.org/poems/55279/ode-to-himself-come-leave-the-loathed-stage Accessed January 9, 2022.

[9] Hoeniger, David. "Gower and Shakespeare in *Pericles.*" *Shakespeare Quarterly.* Vol. 33, No. 4 Oxford University Press, 1982.

[10] Hoeniger, David. "Gower and Shakespeare in *Pericles.*"

[11] Hoeniger, David. "Gower and Shakespeare in *Pericles.*"

[12] Shakespeare, William. *Pericles.* (New Folger's ed.), Washington Square Press/Pocket Books, 2005.

[13] Shakespeare, William. *Pericles.*

[14] Shakespeare, William. *Pericles.*

[15] Shakespeare, William. *Pericles.*

[16] Shakespeare, William. *Pericles.*

[17] Shakespeare, William. *The Taming of the Shrew.* Arden Shakespeare, 2010.

[18] Shakespeare, William. *The Taming of the Shrew.*

[19] "Introduction" *The Taming of the Shrew.* Arden Shakespeare, 2010.

[20] Turner, Robert Y. "The Causal Induction in Some Elizabethan Plays." *Studies in Philology.* Vol. 60, No. 2. University of North Carolina Press, 1963.

[21] Shakespeare, William. *The Taming of the Shrew.* Arden Shakespeare, 2010.

[22] Shakespeare, William. *The Taming of the Shrew.*

[23] Shakespeare, William. *The Taming of the Shrew.*

[24] Shakespeare, William. *The Taming of the Shrew.*

[25] Shakespeare. William. *A Midsummer Night's Dream*. The RSC Shakespeare, 2008.

[26] Shakespeare, William. *The Taming of the Shrew*. Arden Shakespeare, 2010.

[27] Shakespeare, William. *The Taming of the Shrew*.

[28] Shakespeare, William. *The Taming of the Shrew*.

[29] Shakespeare, William. *The Taming of the Shrew*.

[30] Wentersdorf, Karl P. "The Original Ending of *The Taming of the Shrew*: A Reconsideration" *Studies in English Literature 1500-1900*. Vol. 18, No. 2. Rice University, 1978.

[31] Wentersdorf, Karl P. "The Original Ending of The Taming of the Shrew: A Reconsideration."

[32] Hosley, Richard. "Was There a 'Dramatic Epilogue' to *The Taming of the Shrew*?" *Studies in English Literature, 1500-1900*. Vol. 1, No. 2, Rice University, 1961.

[33] Seronsy, Cecil C. "'Supposes' as the Unifying Theme in *The Taming of the Shrew*." *Shakespeare Quarterly*, Vol. 14, No. 1 Oxford University Press, 1963.

[34] Seronsy, Cecil C. "'Supposes' as the Unifying Theme in *The Taming of the Shrew*."

[35] Shakespeare, William. T*he Taming of the Shrew*. Arden Shakespeare, 2010.

[36] Seronsy, Cecil C. "'Supposes' as the Unifying Theme in *The Taming of the Shrew*." *Shakespeare Quarterly*, Vol. 14, No. 1 Oxford University Press, 1963.

[37] Shakespeare, William. T*he Taming of the Shrew*. Arden Shakespeare, 2010.

[38] Shakespeare, William. T*he Taming of the Shrew.*

[39] Shakespeare, William. T*he Taming of the Shrew.*

[40] Shakespeare, William. T*he Taming of the Shrew.*

[41] Shakespeare, William. T*he Taming of the Shrew.*

[42] Bate, Jonathan. *Shakespeare and Ovid.* Clarendon Press, 1992.

[43] Bate, Jonathan. *Shakespeare and Ovid.*

Chapter Five: Ovid

The sexual content and the ambivalent tone of Shakespeare's *Venus and Adonis* shocked early modern readers and marked his work as clearly Ovidian. Frances Meres referred to Shakespeare in 1598 as having the "sweet witty soule of Ovid" (234).[1] And, Gabriel Harvey referred to Edward de Vere as being "nos'd like to Naso" (7)[2] (Ovid's full name was Pūblius Ovidius Nāsō). Jonathan Bate suggests Ovid offered Shakespeare "the things that made him a poet and a dramatist: magic, myth, metamorphosis, rendered with playfulness, verbal dexterity and generic promiscuity" (1).[3] But, he could easily have gleaned these attributes from other classical sources.

Ovid holds a special place in Shakespeare's heart because both poets abhor didacticism. Delacey suggests that Ovid only used ideas as poetic devices, that he "conceived of philosophy not as a perennial search for truth, but rather as a collection of doctrines which could be effectively used on appropriate occasions in literary work" (160).[4] His attitude to ideology is identical to Shakespeare's. Cora Fox quotes Georgia Brown who says Ovidianism "freed literature from the necessity to be didactic" (18).[5] It freed Shakespeare, too.

The *Metamorphoses* is Ovid's retelling of Greek myths. In his essay on *Venus and Adonis*, Bate calls Book Ten — clearly one of Shakespeare's primary sources — "a series of narratives concerning destructive passion and female desire ... [it] teems with aggressive female wooers, and homoerotic charm" (83).[6] Like Shakespeare's plays, these tales, though morally ambivalent, are deeply involving. Bate notes that "when its characters undergo transformations, the language takes the reader along too — we are deluded by Ovid's art into thinking that can feel what it would be like to be, say, a hunted hart or a tree under the axe" (217).[7]

However, Ovid's transformations stand almost aggressively against moralism. The characters are mostly either victims or perpetrators of atrocities like rape or murder. But as Bate notes, instead of offering virtue its reward and evil its punishment, the characters are transformed into other things (non-sentient beings):

> In Ovid, metamorphosis lets the characters off the hook: they are arrested in the moment of intense emotion and released into a vital, vibrant, colourful world of an anthropomorphic nature ... No one is to blame for loving, because one reaches the irresistible conclusion that whichever way you turn, love will destroy you. It is essentially something out of your control. (80-87)[8]

Ovid's love poems are even more morally ambiguous than the *Metamorphoses*. Both *The Art of Love* and *The Remedy of Love* are framed as 'how-to' manuals, and yet thoughtful, considered advice in virtue is the last thing they provide. (It is no accident that, when Lucentio tutors Bianca in Latin in *The Taming of the Shrew,* the text is Ovid's *The Art of Love*.) Alexander Dazell suggests that Ovid frames *The Art of Love* as a guide to seduction, because by creating a thoroughly amoral book of 'rules,' he can easily make fun of didactic poetry: "With a malicious echo of Hesiod, he tells us he will speak the truth, a truth which he has gained from experience and not from the intervention of the gods" (25).[9]

It was in response to the amorality of his work that Ovid was exiled by the Emperor Augustus. And it is Ovid's relentless, unapologetic pragmatism that makes us distrust him. Bate notes that Ovid's advice is still shockingly candid: "Theatre is a good place to take a prospective lover, since 'the rows compel closeness, like it or not, by the conditions of space your girl must be touched'" (15).[10] Ovid also gives suggestions on how to manage simultaneous orgasms during sexual intercourse: "But take care not to crowd on sail and race / Ahead of her, don't fall behind her either; matching pace, / Arrive together at the winning-post In a dead heat."[11] Even an advertisement for the second edition of the 1970s sexual workbook *The Joy of Gay Sex* frames its advice with high moral seriousness — "The authors provide positive and responsible advice on safe sex in all its varieties; on emotional and relationship-oriented issues" (90).[12] In contrast, consider *The Art of Love,* which also advises readers to 'take care' — but in a distinctly amoral way: "Indulge, but secretly veil your sins, with restraint: it's no glory to you to be seeking out wrongdoing. Don't give gifts another girl could spot, or have set times for your assignations. And lest a girl catch you out in your favourite haunts, don't meet all of them in one place."[13]

This marriage of chattiness and moral ambiguity is profoundly discombobulating. Ovid's voice is simultaneously intimate and distant — similar to Shakespeare's voice in *Venus and Adonis* and *The Sonnets.* It's a voice so persuasive we can't resist feeling we are in league with the author — though we are not entirely sure we want to be. In *The Sonnets*, we know what interests the poet, what angers him, obsesses him, and worries him — but Shakespeare gives us only vague, tantalizing hints about the kind of man he might be. In *Venus and Adonis* — though we are entranced — we are ignorant of the narrator's personal opinions about the mess into which these alarmingly unethical gods and mortals have gotten themselves.

Also, Ovid (like the narrator of *The Sonnets*) seems to be tempting us not to trust him by openly denigrating himself. In *The Loves*, the figure of tragedy scolds Ovid: "The matter cramps thy genius, learn to find / manly subject and exert thy mind" (86)[14] — but Ovid is committed to lighter fare: "Gay, wanton, soft, my business is to move / with melting strains, the playful God of love" (86).[15] We *must* question the sincerity of *The Art of Love* and *Remedy of Love* — if only because Ovid's second book blatantly contradicts his first: "I'll now unteach the art I taught before" (206).[16] Just as Shakespeare offers eloquent and moving arguments on both sides of every question, Ovid followed *The Art of Love* — in which he advises the lover never to shine a spotlight on his girlfriend's faults — with *The Remedy of Love* — in which he recommends sex in a sunlit room to kill romance.

What is the point of all this? Well, for one thing, metaphor *itself* is a kind of metamorphosis. The gods who transform people into beasts and flowers in myth are like the poet who transforms ideas into images, images into stories, and experience into metaphor. In this sense, all Ovid's work is functionally aesthetic. The changes that happen to the characters in Ovid's retelling of the Greek myths are a physical embodiment of the process of poetry. The only thing that we 'learn' by example from Ovid is how to turn 'real life' into fiction.

Shakespeare's numerous mentions of Ovid indicate he is obsessed with his literary forefather. He treats Ovid as one might treat an old friend, mentioning him sometimes in reverent tribute and at other times with a gentle satirical nudge. When Tranio arrives in Padua in *The Taming of the Shrew,* he sings Ovid's praises: "Let's be no stoics nor no stocks I pray / Or so devout to Aristotle's checks / As Ovid be an outcast quite abjured" (1.1.31-33).[17] But Malvolio in *Twelfth Night* critiques the *Metamorphoses*:

> CLOWN: What is the opinion of Pythagoras concerning wild fowl?
>
> MALVOLIO: That the soul of our grandam might haply inhabit a bird.
>
> CLOWN: What thinkest thou of his opinion?
>
> MALVOLIO: I think nobly of the soul, and no way approve his opinion. (4.2.52-58)[18]

This cutting reference is to Pythagoras' theory of reincarnation as represented by Ovid: "Everything changes, nothing dies: the spirit wanders ... passing from a wild beast into a human being, from our body into a beast, but is never destroyed."[19]

Shakespeare's obsession with Ovid is not just exemplified by the sheer volume of his allusions to him, but also by the fact that they take so many forms. *The Winter's Tale* features an appropriation of Ovidian myth that holds pride of place in the plot: the statue of Hermione that springs to life is a dramatization of the story of Pygmalion. But there is also an infamous, brief stage direction for Antigonus: "He exits, pursued by a bear" (3.3.64).[20] Bate reveals this was a reference to Callisto, a woman in the *Metamorphoses* transformed into a bear. Shakespeare's reference to Pygmalion is clear and calculated, but if the 'bear' is indeed an allusion to Ovid, it seems unconscious — axiomatic even — as if Ovid was always in the back of Shakespeare's mind.

As Bate so assiduously observes, Shakespeare's work is peppered everywhere with Ovidianisms. But two of Shakespeare's plays stand out as being particularly dominated by Ovid's work. Katherine Blakeney notes: "*Titus Andronicus* and *A Midsummer Night's Dream* include the most direct references to Ovid, re-telling the stories of Philomel, and Pyramus and Thisbe."[21]

In *Titus Andronicus*, Titus' daughter, Lavinia, suffers a fate similar to Philomela's in the *Metamorphoses*. Blakeney notes she "is so entrenched in her archetype that she is hardly an independent character at all."[22] Lavinia's fate in *Titus Andronicus* is slightly different than Philomela's — but similar enough to telegraph that the character is a variation on Ovid's heroine. When Tamora's sons, Chiron and Demetrius, rape Lavinia, Tamora's lover, Aaron, says: "This is the day of doom for Bassianus. / His Philomel must lose her tongue today. / Thy sons make pillage of her chastity" (2.3.42-44).[23]

Chiron and Demetrius chop off Lavinia's hands so she will be unable to weave their names into a tapestry as Philomela did to her molesters, thus, as Leon Grek observes, showing "themselves to be attentive readers of the *Metamorphoses*" (20).[24] If that is not enough, Lavinia — sans tongue and hands — explains her rape and mutilation by designating the relevant plot points in a copy of Ovid's poem. Finally, as Grek says, "while the Goths use the *Metamorphoses* as a handbook for rape, Titus uses it as a manual for revenge" (20).[25] In order to wreak revenge on Tamora, Titus (like Procne in Ovid's poem) serves her slaughtered sons to Tamora for dinner. He tells the boys (before killing them) that he will "make two pasties of your shameful heads / And bid that strumpet, your unhallowed dam / Like to the earth swallow her own increase" (5.2.193-95).[26]

Grek suggests *Titus Andronicus* was written when Shakespeare was young, and he "would have been aware that the reading of Ovid was contested between those who saw it as entertaining literature and those who saw it as a guide to practical matters in contemporary daily life" (19).[27] Grek elaborates:

> In their interpretative approach to Ovid, then, both Romans and Goths align themselves with the moralizing tradition of Ovidian interpretation. Like the moralizers, the characters of

> *Titus* treat *Metamorphoses* as a didactic text, with practical value for the conduct of contemporary life. In *Titus*, this functionalist reading of Ovid has dire consequences. Rather than providing characters with moral wisdom, Ovid furnishes them with justifications and instructions for horrifically immoral actions. (20)[28]

Since the central activity of the plot primarily involves relentless vengeance, some think *Titus Andronicus* is pointing to the uselessness of revenge. But does Shakespeare need to drag us through five acts of this carnage — some of it ridiculous in its extremity — in order to make his point? Grek believes Shakespeare turns our attention to Ovid in *Titus Andronicus* to remind us that, although a poem may provide inspiration and even redemption, its 'message' cannot be directly translated into action.

When Grek speaks of young Shakespeare's reaction to the 'moralizing tradition of Ovidian interpretation,' he is referring to a practice that originated in the 14th century with a French document called *Ovide Moralisé*. About a fifth of *Ovide Moralisé* (attributed to an anonymous Franciscan friar) is a translation of Ovid's *Metamorphoses.* The rest is religious exegesis — a Christian analysis of Ovid's work offering pious readers permission to enjoy the scandalous text. *Ovide Moralisé* inaugurated a medieval treatment of Ovid's poem that extended into the early modern period.

The culmination of the Elizabethan tradition of *Ovide Moralisé* is Arthur Golding's translation of Ovid's *Metamorphoses*. Bate tells us that as early as 1767, the scholar Richard Farmer "showed that Shakespeare used Thomas North's translation of Plutarch and Arthur Golding's of Ovid" (7).[29] Bate thinks that Golding's translation "probably continued Shakespeare's only sustained direct confrontation with the moralizing tradition" (31).[30] That Shakespeare had knowledge of Golding's translation is obvious; after all, both Shakespeare's plays and Golding's translation are part of what Bate calls "a significant part of a post-reformation project to establish England as a Protestant nation with its own high culture" (30).[31] Bate notes that the text was made more 'English' through the addition of words and atmosphere — in the same manner that Shakespeare gave his Italian plays an 'English' aspect through detail and word usage.

Grek quotes Ettin: "The tradition of *Ovide moralisé*— of which Golding was a part — was intrinsically false to the experience of reading Ovid, false even to the nature of the stories themselves" (23).[32] As Furey notes, Golding's preparatory epistle and the preface to his translation ask us to read Ovid's violent, sexual, pagan story as a Christian allegory: "I would not wish the simple sort offended for too bee" (326).[33] And in Nims' version of Golding's translation, apparently, it is clear Golding wishes to inform us that the references to pagan gods in the text are not what they appear: "Must wee thinke the learned men that did theis names frequent, some further things and purposes by those devises ment. By Jove and Juno understand all states of princely port: By Ops and Saturne auncient folke that are of elder sort" (424),[34] Furey also notes that Golding suggests that although Ovid makes no mention of God, he *would have* done so— that is if our Christian God had existed for him — "The trewe and everliving God the Paynims did not knowe: Which caused them the name of Godds on creatures too bestowe" (326).[35]

Critics have laughed at Golding's unsuccessful attempt to impose moralism on Ovid's tales. Lyne scoffs, for instance, at the idea that Daphne's transformation into a tree is a reward: "The idea that it is through chastity that Daphne wins 'everlasting fame and immorality' is an awkward one" (50).[36] Cirillo says that in Renaissance myth — and in Ovid's original text — "'the form of the hermaphrodite was uniquely that of perfect love because it alone imaged the mystic union wherein the two sexes became one self-sufficient sex that contains both'" (62).[37] In contrast, Bate says, "Golding moralised the fate of the hermaphrodite as a warning against effeminacy" (61).[38]

It's likely Shakespeare would have had very mixed feelings about Golding's *Metamorphoses.* Though undoubtedly he would have admired Golding's dedication to the creation of a British culture, evident in this noble attempt to translate Ovid from the Latin into what was then known as 'the vulgar,' Golding's pompous moralizing would likely have irked him. Or perhaps it might have done more than that. Could Golding's Ovid have angered Shakespeare *so very much* he was inspired to write *Titus Andronicus?* Was Shakespeare's diatribe against didacticism aimed directly at Arthur Golding? This idea might seem far-fetched. Unless, of course, Ovid's *Metamorphoses* was not translated by Arthur Golding, *but by a young William Shakespeare.*

This scenario is not quite as bizarre as it sounds. Golding's translation was published in 1567 when Edward de Vere was 17 years old. As a ward of Queen Elizabeth in late summer of 1564, de Vere lived with William Cecil, Lord Burghley, and had easy access to one of the largest libraries in England. He was soon to be awarded an honorary Masters degree at Cambridge — and, (as Mark Anderson points out) the academic standard required for an honorary degree was, at that time, quite high. By 1567, de Vere matriculated at the principal law school in London: Gray's Inn. Of course, that de Vere was a well educated young man does not prove that he is the real translator of Golding's Ovid. But think again. Arthur Golding was Edward de Vere's uncle. And Mark Anderson mentions that three years before Golding's *Metamorphoses* was published, Golding wrote a letter to his nephew, praising his erudition:

> It is not unknown to others, and I have had experience thereof myself, how earnest a desire your Honor hath naturally grafted in you to read, peruse and communicate with others as well the histories of ancient times, and things done long ago, as also of the present estate of things in our days — and that not without a certain pregnancy of wit and ripeness of understanding. (27)[39]

This might simply be a fond uncle's peon to a surprisingly gifted child poet. Or, it might be a not too subtle hint that Golding's nephew was the real translator of the *Metamorphoses*. If he was the translator, even a young Earl of Oxford would not have been permitted to reveal it, for artistic endeavours were considered inappropriate for noblemen. *The Arte of English Poesie* (1589) specifically mentions de Vere in this respect: "Courtly makers, noblemen ... who have written excellently well, as it would appear if their doings could be found out and made public with the rest. Of which number is first that noble gentleman Edward Earl of Oxford" (306).[40]

Golding's introduction and the poem itself make an incongruous pair; the introduction is as intent on moralizing as the poem itself is not. Lyne notes that "only on a few occasions does a genuinely moralising tone enter the narrative" (30).[41] Why would Golding — so desperately dedicated to wrenching a lesson out of a poem where none can be found — have given us a translation of Ovid that is completely faithful to the original in tone, revelling in its fundamentally ambivalent, nay — quite amoral — sensibility?

To top it all off, Golding was a pious Protestant — deeply religious, a Calvinist, and as Richard M. Waugaman reminds us:

> John F. Nims, in his Introduction to Ovid's Metamorphoses, the Arthur Golding Translation 1567, muses about the flagrant paradox of Golding, the "convinced Puritan who spent much of his life translating the sermons and commentaries of John Calvin" undertaking to English this work of Ovid, "the sophisticated darling of a dissolute society, the author of a scandalous handbook of seduction" [i.e., *The Art of Love*]. (8)[42]

There is much circumstantial evidence pointing to de Vere — and away from Golding — as the true translator. Golding never again translated anything like the *Metamorphoses,* and when he was supposed to be working on the translation of it, he was also completing John Brende's translation of *Caesar's Gallic War* (under pressure from Lord Burghley). Meanwhile we know that Shakespeare is likely to have mastered Latin — because in *A Midsummer Night's Dream*, he uses the name 'Titania,' which is in the original Latin *Metamorphoses*, but not in Golding. Though it is unlikely that 'the Man from Stratford' read Ovid in the original Latin, the same cannot be said of Edward de Vere.

If that is not enough, Waugaman notices the overwhelming presence of one of Shakespeare's favourite poetic figures in Golding's translation: "Gordon Braden notes that Golding did not use as much hendiadys (which he calls 'doublets') in his later works. Yet in 'his' Ovid, 'he often renders a single Latin word twice or more'" (12).[43] We are all very familiar with one of Shakespeare's favourite rhetorical figures called hendiadys: i.e. the use of two adjectives or nouns instead of one. Hamlet's "the slings and arrows of outrageous fortune" (3.1. 66),[44] is one example — Macbeth's "It is a tale / Told by an idiot, full of sound and fury" (5.5. 29-30)[45] is another. Shakespeare's fondness for hendiadys is consistent with his compulsive Gorgian affection for antithetical figures (like paradox, alliteration, repetition and puns). Waugaman notes, astutely, that "as when he repeats a single word in his plays because it has a different nuance each time, he is asking us to notice different shades of meaning in the words that he pairs" (18).[46]

Lyne mentions "Ovid's Metamorphoses roams through the known world, without reflected different dialects; but when Golding came to translate it, he added "linguistic variation at several points" (56).[47] So, "'the case of 'Iche', used instead of Golding's usual 'I'; during the Renaissance [...] was identified with West Country speech."[48] The disguised god Mercury — also in the Golding translation — has a similar accent. The god Mercury was associated with Shakespeare and eloquence. *Coincidentally* — or perhaps not — Edgar in *King Lear* — is disguised (like Mercury in Golding's translation) — and uses the same West Country accent: "Keep out, / che vore ye, or Ise try whether your costard or my / ballow be the harder. Chill be plain with you" (4.6. 269-71).[49]

But as convincing as all this might be, the real proof that Shakespeare is the author of Golding's translation lies in the loving homage to Ovid that is constituted by *A Midsummer Night's Dream.* Madeleine Forey tells us that in this play Shakespeare "made substantial borrowings from Golding's translation, some of which have not yet been recognized" (321).[50] In *A Midsummer Night's Dream*, a tribe of 'rude mechanicals' enact a scene from Ovid's *Metamorphoses* — the tragedy of Pyramus and Thisbe. Forey continues: "Several critics have insisted that the mechanicals' interlude parodies Golding's style, a style that by the 1590s was both very familiar and very old-fashioned, and hence laughable" (321).[51] She states more specifically that "Robert F. Willson argues 'Pyramus and Thisbe' mocks both the 'jog trot rhythm of Golding's fourteeners', whose rhythm is inappropriate to the sentiments expressed, and Golding's excessive alliteration, assonance, and apostrophe" (324).[52]

Bottom's introduction to the 'play within the play' seems to be making a direct reference to Golding's didacticism: "We are not here. That you should here repent you" (5.1.119).[53] Bottom's garbled syntax changes the meaning of what he intends to say, and in the process speaks volumes about the relationship between style and content. He means to say that they are not there to teach the audience anything — 'we are not here that we should repent you,' but the added period seems to suggest that the actors don't exist. This brings to mind Gorgias' assertion that 'nothing exists,' but also reminds us there is a certain ontological uncertainty on the part of the characters in *any* play. Well, of course the characters in a play do not really exist. They are, as Puck tells us in his epilogue, only a dream. When Puck mentions 'offence' in his final speech, this echoes Golding's introduction. For in order to reassure the audience, he must make it clear that the characters in the play are not real:

> If we shadows have offended,
> Think but this, and all is mended—
> That you have but slumbered here
> While these visions did appear.
> And this weak and idle theme,
> No more yielding but a dream. (5.1.415-19)[54]

Why are the actors concerned we will think they are real? It's because actors sometimes believe too much — not only in a narcissistic way— not only in their own expertise as actors — but in the potency of the reality they create, and its power to replace the day to day world.

In fact, the rude mechanicals *are* terribly worried that ladies in the audience will mistake Snug for a real lion. Bottom comes up with a perfect solution, one that is meta-theatrical, to say the least. Snug will keep assuring the audience he is not a lion, and that he does not wish to hurt them — because he is really only Snug:

> Nay, you must name his name, and half his face must be seen through the lion's neck. And he himself must speak through, saying thus — or to the same defect — "Ladies," or "Fair ladies," "I would wish you" or "I would request you" or "I would entreat you" "not to fear, not to tremble, my life for yours. If you think I come hither as a lion, it were pity of my life. No, I am no such thing. I am a man as other men are." And there indeed let him name his name, and tell them plainly he is Snug the joiner. (3.1. 33-41)[55]

This is perhaps why we are so very fond of the rude mechanicals, and when they leave the stage, we are sad to see them go. In the end, it is not just the actors' mistaken belief in their own artistry, but their unshakeable belief in art; something that seems bestowed upon them by the simple audacity of partaking in this comic monstrosity that manages to carry us away, despite ourselves. The rude mechanicals believe in themselves — and in the play — so much that, like Sly in *The Taming of the Shrew*, they come to confuse real life and fantasy.

Their unassailable faith in their own acting talent convinces their audience, too. But of what? When Pyramus discovers a dead Thisbe, Hippolyta cries, "Beshrew my heart, but I pity the man" (5.1. 286)[56] — meaning on the face of it that though Hippolyta may not pity *Thisbe*, she pities *Bottom* for believing he is a peerless performer, when clearly, he is not.

Theseus suggests that it is the belief that the actors have in their own talent that makes them admirable:

> THESEUS: The best in this kind are but shadows; and the worst are no worse, if imagination amend them.
> HIPPOLYTA: It must be your imagination then, and not theirs.
> THESEUS: If we imagine no worse of them than they of themselves, they may pass for excellent men. (5.1. 214-19)[57]

It is the belief that art gives us, the magic it imposes upon us, that we cherish, and indeed this is the reason that we love the rude mechanicals so very, very much. The upshot is that what we create when we make a play — or even just watch a play — is ourselves. The work of art must not attempt to teach us anything, but instead, by testing our belief in an alternative reality, it may facilitate the creation of who we are. Indeed, a poem must stand on its own two feet; it requires no justification. Bottom says, "The actors are at hand, and by their show. You shall know all that you are like to know" (5.1.120-21).[58] In this way, Shakespeare offers us no less, and yet, somehow, considerably more, than just a story.

Endnotes

1 Jackson, MacD. P. "Francis Meres and the Cultural Contexts of Shakespeare's Rival Poet Sonnets." *The Review of English Studies.* Vol. 56, No. 224. Oxford University Press, 2005.

2 Ray, William. "The Factual Desert of Stanley Wells." https://www.academia.edu/7496645/The_Factual_Desert_of_Stanley_Wells

3 Bate, Jonathan. *How the Classics Made Shakespeare.* Princeton University Press, 2020.

[4] DeLacy, Phillip. "Philosophical Doctrine and Poetic Technique in Ovid." *The Classical Journal* Vol. 43 No. 3. The Classical Association of the Midwest and South, Inc., 1947.

[5] Fox, Cora. *Ovid and the Politics of Emotion in Elizabethan England.* Palgrave and MacMillan, 2009.

[6] Bate, Jonathan. *Shakespeare and Ovid.* Oxford University Press, 1993.

[7] Bate, Jonathan. *Shakespeare and Ovid.*

[8] Bate, Jonathan. *Shakespeare and Ovid.*

[9] Dazell, Alexander. *The Criticism of Didactic Poetry: Essays on Lucretius, Virgil, and Ovid.*

[10] Bate, Jonathan. *Shakespeare and Ovid.* Oxford University Press, 1993.

[11] "Ars amatoria: Controversial advice on sex and date rape from Rome" *Books On Trial*. https://www.booksontrial.com/ars-amatoria-art-of-love-ovid-controversial-advice/

[12] *The Joy of Gay Sex*. *Amazon.ca.* https://www.amazon.ca/Joy-Gay-Sex-revised-expanded/*dp/0060012749.*

[13] Ovid. "The Art of Love" *Poetry in Translation.* https://www.poetryintranslation.com/PITBR/Latin/ArtofLoveBkII.php

[14] Ovid. *Love Poems.* Wordsworth Editions Ltd., 2003.

[15] Ovid. *Love Poems.*

[16] Ovid. *Love Poems.*

[17] Shakespeare, William. T*he Taming of the Shrew*. Arden Shakespeare, 2010.

[18] Shakespeare, William. *Twelfth Night*. (New Folger's ed.), Washington Square Press/Pocket Books, 1993.

[19] Ovid. "Metamorphoses." *Metamorphoses Book XV* (A.S. Kline's Version) https://ovid.lib.virginia.edu/trans/Metamorph15.htm Accessed January 19, 2022.

[20] Shakespeare. William. *A Winter's Tale.* (New Folger's ed.), Washington Square Press/Pocket Books, 1998.

[21] Blakeney, Katherine. "Ovid's Metamorphoses and the Plays of Shakespeare" *Inquiries*. http://www.inquiriesjournal.com/articles/105/2/ovids-metamorphoses-and-the-plays-of-shakespeare vol 1 #12, 2009.

[22] Blakeney, Katherine. "Ovid's Metamorphoses and the Plays of Shakespeare"

[23] Shakespeare, William. *Titus Andronicus.* (New Folger's ed.), Washington Square Press/Pocket Books, 2005.

[24] Grek, Leon. "Performing Ovid's *Metamorphoses* in *Titus Andronicus* and *A Midsummer Night's Dream*" *McGill Classical Studies*. Vol 7. McGill University, 2008-2009. https://www.mcgill.ca/classics/teaching/hirundo/volume07.

[25] Grek, Leon. "Performing Ovid's *Metamorphoses* in *Titus Andronicus* and *A Midsummer Night's Dream*".

[26] Shakespeare, William. *Titus Andronicus.* (New Folger's ed.), Washington Square Press/Pocket Books, 2005.

[27] Grek, Leon. "Performing Ovid's *Metamorphoses* in *Titus Andronicus* and *A Midsummer Night's Dream*," *McGill Classical Studies*. Vol 7. McGill University, 2008-2009. https://www.mcgill.ca/classics/teaching/hirundo/volume07.

[28] Grek, Leon. "Performing Ovid's *Metamorphoses* in *Titus Andronicus* and *A Midsummer Night's Dream*".

[29] Bate, Jonathan. *Shakespeare and Ovid.* Oxford University Press, 1993.

[30] Bate, Jonathan. *Shakespeare and Ovid.*

[31] Bate, Jonathan. *Shakespeare and Ovid.*

[32] Grek, Leon. "Performing Ovid's *Metamorphoses* in *Titus Andronicus* and *A Midsummer Night's Dream*" *McGill Classical Studies*. Vol 7. McGill University, 2008-2009. https://www.mcgill.ca/classics/teaching/hirundo/volume07.

[33] Forey, Madeleine. "Bless thee, Bottom, bless thee! Thou Art Translated!": Ovid, Golding, and *A Midsummer Night's Dream.*

The Modern Language Review. Vol. 94, No. 2. Modern Humanities Research Association, 1998.

[34] Nims, John Frederik, *Ovid's Metamorphoses The Arthur Golding Translation 1567* Paul Dry Books, 2000.

[35] Forey, Madeleine. "Bless thee, Bottom, bless thee! Thou Art Translated!": Ovid, Golding, and *A Midsummer Night's Dream. The Modern Language Review.* Vol. 93, No. 2. Modern Humanities Research Association, 1998.

[36] Lyne, Rafael. *Ovid's Changing Worlds: English Metamorphoses 1567-1632.* Oxford University Press, 2004.

[37] Cirillo, A.R. "The Fair Hermaphrodite: Love-Union in the Poetry of Donne and Spenser" *Studies in English Literature*, 1500-1900 Vol. 9, No. 1. 1969, Rice University.

[38] Bate, Jonathan. *Shakespeare and Ovid.* Oxford University Press, 1993.

[39] Anderson, Mark. *Shakespeare By Another Name*. Gotham Books, 2005.

[40] Ward, B.M. "The Authorship of the Arte of English Poesie: A Suggestion". *The Re-view of English Studies*. Vol. 1, No. 3 Oxford University Press, 1925.

[41] Lyne, Rafael. *Ovid's Changing Worlds: English Metamorphoses 1567-1632.* Oxford University Press, 2004.

[42] Waugaman, Richard M. "Did Edward de Vere Translate Ovid's *Metamorphoses*?" *The Oxfordian.* Shakespeare Oxford Fellowship, 2018.

[43] Waugaman, Richard M. "Did Edward de Vere Translate Ovid's *Metamorphoses*?"

[44] Shakespeare, William. *Hamlet*. (New Folger's ed.), Washington Square Press/Pocket Books, 2012.

[45] Shakespeare, William. *Macbeth*. (New Folger's ed.), Washington Square Press/Pocket Books, 2013.

[46] Waugaman, Richard M. "Did Edward de Vere Translate Ovid's *Metamorphoses*?" *The Oxfordian* Shakespeare Oxford Fellowship, 2018.

[47] Lyne, Rafael. *Ovid's Changing Worlds: English Metamorphoses 1567-1632.* Oxford University Press, 2004.

[48] Lyne, Rafael. *Ovid's Changing Worlds: English Metamorphoses 1567-1632.*

[49] Shakespeare, William. *King Lear*. (New Folger's ed.), Washington Square Press/Pocket Books, 2004.

[50] Foray, Madeleine. "Bless thee, Bottom, bless thee! Thou Art Translated!" Ovid, Golding, and *A Midsummer Night's Dream*. *The Modern Language Review.* Vol. 93, No. 2. Modern Humanities Research Association, 1998.

[51] Foray, Madeleine. "Bless thee, Bottom, bless thee! Thou Art Translated!" Ovid, Golding, and *A Midsummer Night's Dream*.

[52] Foray, Madeleine. "Bless thee, Bottom, bless thee! Thou Art Translated!" Ovid, Golding, and *A Midsummer Night's Dream*.

[53] Shakespeare, William. *A Midsummer Night's Dream*. Royal Shakespeare Company, 2008.

[54] Shakespeare, William. *A Midsummer Night's Dream*.

[55] Shakespeare, William. *A Midsummer Night's Dream*.

[56] Shakespeare, William. *A Midsummer Night's Dream*.

[57] Shakespeare, William. *A Midsummer Night's Dream*.

[58] Shakespeare, William. *A Midsummer Night's Dream*.

Chapter Six: Pain

Shakespeare was a master rhetorician whose poetry was about poetry; but, it was not only about that. He wrote not only to address — but to remedy — a very deep personal pain. His work, paradoxically, not only teaches us that art should not teach, but that instead, art comes from a deeper place: a cause that is not always explicable to either the writer or the audience.

There are many suggestions in Shakespeare's work that he viewed art as having healing powers. Sly in *The Taming of the Shrew* is told theatre "bars a thousand harms and lengthens life" (Induction. 2.133).[1] This information is framed in medical jargon: "For so your doctors hold it very meet / Seeing too much sadness has congealed your blood, / And melancholy is the nurse of frenzy" (Induction. 2.127-29).[2] Here, Shakespeare references Aristotle's catharsis, invoking a medical process: the purgation of pity and fear. The viewer is, in effect, being 'bled' of emotion.

In this way, Shakespeare seems, uncharacteristically, to agree with Aristotle and stands in opposition to Plato, who admitted (as Timothy W. Burns observes) — with some embarrassment — that poetry was a guilty pleasure because the poet is "indeed capable of the difficult task of imitating the prudent and quiet character. But when it happens, the prudent and quiet character is not easily understood by 'the many'" (332).[3] Poetry is dangerous because it "can make those who feed their souls with it so soft as to be incapable of accepting what is" (332),[4] and its "charms feed a strong pull away from what reason says is beneficial or advantageous" (336).[5]

In other words, poetry causes us to wallow in feeling. Despite Plato's proclamation, Shakespeare gives us many hints that he is much less interested in philosophy than he is in emotion. In an essay on Shakespeare and Seneca, Patrick Gray lists the various instances in which Shakespeare's characters refuse a philosophical solution. Leonato in *Much Ado About Nothing* says: "No man's virtue nor sufficiency / To be so moral when he shall endure /The like himself. Therefore give me no counsel" (5.1.27-31).[6] Romeo rejects Friar Laurence's philosophical advice: "Unless philosophy can make a Juliet, / Displant a town, reverse a prince's doom, / It helps not, it prevails not; talk no more" (3.3.61–63).[7] And there is Hamlet's famous admonition to Horatio that "There are more things in heaven and earth, Horatio, / Than are dreamt of in your philosophy" (1.5.187-88).[8]

Seneca was a Roman 'closet' dramatist and rhetorician; there is evidence from Shakespeare's work that he had undoubtedly read Seneca's plays. Gray contrasts Seneca's treatment of emotion with Shakespeare's: "Seneca's tragedies are designed to illustrate the disastrous effects of unchecked emotion" (218),[9] whereas, "the height of human dignity, as Shakespeare sees it, is ... to give up the Senecan dream of self-mastery" (215).[10] Shakespeare's characters wallow in pain. Hamlet is flamboyantly consumed with melancholy, Richard II seriously considers digging a grave with his own tears, and Titus goes on and on about the burdensome dampness of sorrow: "In summer's drought I'll drop upon thee still; / In winter with warm tears I'll melt the snow" (3.1.19-20).[11]

McGilchrist suggests that "an interesting study could be made of the place of tears in the art and poetry in the [early modern] period — in the plays of Shakespeare, in the songs of Dowland ..." (306).[12] Now, certainly, many of Shakespeare's characters have good reason to cry — Titus lost his children, Richard II lost his kingdom, and Hamlet lost his father. But Antonio in *The Merchant of Venice* is sad for no reason at all:

> In sooth I know no why I am so sad,
> It wearies me, you say it wearies you
> But how I caught it, found it, or came by it,
> What stuff 'tis made of, whereof it is born
> I am to learn. (1.1.1-5)[13]

Like the melancholy Jaques, there seems to almost be a joy mixed in with the experience of pain; this was called melancholy. McGilchrist thinks "that sadness and pleasure intermingled was hardly accepted until the Renaissance" (307).[14]

Jaques is consumed with unremitting grief over a wounded stag in *As You Like It.*

His obsession might seem a joke on his sentimental nature; it is much more than that. He says of the stag: "And thus the hairy fool, / Much marked of the melancholy Jaques / Stood on th'extremest verge of the swift brook, / Augmenting it with tears" (2.1.41-44).[15] Jaques even moralizes that we "are mere usurpers, tyrants, and what's worse, / To fright the animals and to kill them up / In their assigned and native dwelling place" (2.1. 64-66).[16]

Shakespeare was no animal rights activist. Indeed, his sympathy for helpless and abused animals is one with this sympathy for helpless and abused women. *The Rape of Lucrece* and *Titus Andronicus* both focus on the trauma of a wounded female victim. No violated heroine in early modern literature can compare with Lucrece. Her response to rape is articulated with singular psychological insight, taking her through eleven stages of grief. First, she wants to rip away her flesh; then she curses the night and blames herself; then she curses chance, opportunity, and time — and, finally, her rapist, Tarquin. She opines that "this helpless smoke of words does me no right" and decides "the remedy is to ... let forth my soul defiled by blood" (298).[17] However, she can't find a knife to do the deed, and waffles between life and death, finally killing herself, because in doing so "my shame is dead, my honour is reborn" (306).[18]

Similarly, Lavinia's suffering after her rape in *Titus Andronicus* is chronicled with precision. Her grotesque mutilation by Demetrius and Chiron might seem, in itself, to be sufficient —that is, a potent comment on masculine brutality. But, is Lavinia actually silenced by having her tongue cut out? For just as Othello aestheticizes his cruel error, Lavinia aestheticizes her rape by attempting to act it out for her father utilizing the text of Ovid's *Metamorphoses,* thus turning it into a performance. Deborah Willis, quoting Mary Laughlin Fawcett, says: "Her silence after her humiliation appears to be a development, an increase in eloquence, rather than a stopping or reversal" (43).[19] And, though Titus murders her at the end of the play, "yet in a peculiar way Titus seems to be critiquing the ideology of rape" (49-50).[20]

Shakespeare's obsession with the pain — and his insistence on offering women the opportunity to expose their feelings in excruciating detail — has its origins in Ovid's *Metamorphoses,* and *Heroides,* Both feature violated, grieving heroines gifted with a startling eloquence. Cora Fox notes that in Ovid, "female emotions, themselves associated with change, are given special prominence" (3).[21] Fox thinks Ovid's habit of giving voice to the voiceless is fundamentally anti-authoritarian: "Unlike ... Plato and Seneca, Ovid's works are insistently literary and in fact non-systematizing ... less clearly marked as engaged in intellectual or ideational negations, but ... are equally central to the construction of culture" (5). [22] The fact that Ovid's works have often been dismissed as being 'pretty stories' — or, paradoxically, as pornography — is symptomatic of a culture that demands art be transparently didactic. In contrast, both Ovid and Shakespeare transmit radical messages through form.

Shakespeare is interested in women's voices because he is obsessed with those who have difficulty — for whatever reason — expressing pain, and difficulty finding those who will listen. His characters often remark on the difficulty of putting their grief into words. Bushy in *Richard II* delivers a complex monologue on this very subject when trying to comfort the queen — telling her that the prism of tears turns grief into a mere shadow of itself:

> Each substance of a grief hath twenty shadows,
> Which shows like grief itself, but is not so.
> For sorrow's eye, glazed with blinding tears,
> Divides one thing entire to many objects;
> Like perspectives, which rightly gazed upon
> Show nothing but confusion, eyed awry
> Distinguish form: so your sweet majesty,
> Looking awry upon your lord's departure,
> Find shapes of grief, more than himself, to wail;
> Which, look'd on as it is, is nought but shadows
> Of what it is not. Then, thrice-gracious queen,
> More than your lord's departure weep not: more's not seen;
> Or if it be, 'tis with false sorrow's eye,
> Which for things true weeps things imaginary. (2.2.14-28)[23]

After his deposition, a deeply despondent Richard II finds he is unable to look at himself in a cracked mirror. Bolingbroke suggests, "The shadow of your sorrow hath destroy'd the shadow of your face" (4.1.303-04).[24] Richard II is taken with this metaphor, further relishing and aestheticizing his pain:

> Say that again.
> The shadow of my sorrow! ha! let's see:
> Tis very true, my grief lies all within;
> And these external manners of laments
> Are merely shadows to the unseen grief
> That swells with silence in the tortured soul. (4.1.305-10)[25]

Hamlet is troubled by the same contradiction, for though he believes his sorrow over his father's death is deep, he laments that an actor in a play is more convincing than he is when expressing pain: "For Hecuba! / What's Hecuba to him or he to (Hecuba) /That he should weep for her?" (2.2.585-87).[26]

But the essential contradiction (there must always be a contradiction!) is that though articulating our grief is impossible, it nevertheless *must be expressed.* Expressions of deep feeling are often misunderstood because they cannot find adequate expression in words. This is a torturous paradox: we are compelled to explicate our grief — describe it, explain it, exactly — and yet, inevitably, we cannot. When Titus' brother, Marcus, discovers the mute, mutilated Lavinia, he observes, "Sorrow concealed, like an oven stopp'd, / Doth burn the heart to cinders" (2.4.36-37).[27]

Shakespeare's observation about this paradox — the twinned necessity and difficulty of expressing trauma — resembles the post-structuralist response to the Holocaust. Adorno's quite famous (and often misquoted) notion is that "after Auschwitz, to write a poem is barbaric" (34).[28] Adorno observed that any poetic depiction of any atrocity distorts, and/or trivializes the horror, making it unrecognizable.

Jean François Lyotard in *The Differend* reminds us of "the case of the French Holocaust denier Robert Faurisson, who claimed that the only testimony he would accept would be that of someone who had actually been through the gas chambers."[29] By citing Fauisson's offensive paradox, Lyotard means to say that the pain endured by victims of the Holocaust is impossible to put into words. He reminds us that "to the privation constituted by the damage there is added the impossibility of bringing it to the knowledge of others."[30]

The tension between the urgency of expressing an emotion and the impossibility of doing so is a profound aesthetic dilemma. But this problem may also be a spur to creation. Sontag argues that oppressed peoples are the motor behind modern art: "Jews and homosexuals are the outstanding creative minorities in contemporary urban culture" (290).[31] The blues — and the jazz form itself — are thought to be directly descended from Negro spirituals; certainly, neither of these musical forms can be separated from the oppression of Black people. In his stand-up comedy routine, Chris Rock reminds us that Black slaves in America were punished for reading. The Nazis burned books by Jews. The plays of gay writers Tennessee Williams, Edward Albee, and William Inge were excoriated by homophobic theatre critics like Stanley Kauffman and Howard Taubman. Still, these minorities managed to create much of what we recognize as modern culture.

Though the relentlessly persecuted suffer endlessly, their singular triumph is that they are able to transform their experience into art. Could it be precisely *because* they are ridiculed, ignored, or even forbidden to do so? Certainly, no one in his or her right mind *wishes* to be oppressed. But one might be forgiven for wondering if being part of an oppressed minority offers a cultural advantage. What is there about feeling compelled to express pain — while simultaneously being denied the opportunity — that summons eloquence? Is oppression itself an aesthetic aphrodisiac?

And what does all this have to do with Shakespeare?

Ironically, those who insist Shakespeare was the Man from Stratford speak of a life not only uncrowded by incident, but a life that was 'normal' to an almost absurd degree. Scholars search high and low for the source of the Stratford grain dealer's inspiration. The best they can come up with is the possibility that he was obligated to marry his slightly older wife, Ann Hathaway, because she was pregnant; or that he and Anne had marital problems because he disappeared for seven years to London; or that he was traumatized by the death of his son, Hamnet. Even less convincing as fodder for genius are the tedious tales of the man from Stratford's money-lending debacles, the tiresome lawsuits and debts. But when the fact that Shakespeare, upon his death, left his wife his 'second best bed' is debated — as if it was *a curse from beyond the grave* — it all seems a little hopeless, like grasping at straws.

Artists are not required to lead troubled lives — although they often do. Great novels can rise from a paucity of experience. T.S. Eliot worked in a bank. Proust lived most of his life confined to a sick-bed. He, nevertheless, managed to convince us in *Remembrance of Things Past* that his longing for a 'madeleine' dipped in lime blossom was both traumatic and deeply touching. The notion that artists must necessarily lead complex lives that climax in heroic suffering all but disappeared after the 19th century.

Yet certain images from Shakespeare's work haunt us so much that we can't help but wonder if they also haunted him. These are the images we would rather *un*-remember. When Ross in *Macbeth* speaks of the strange behaviour of the horses after the murder of King Duncan, an 'Old Man' murmurs quietly, "Tis said they eat each / other" (4.2.24-25).[32] What? Where did that image come from? Alexander Leggatt mentions similar images of arresting horror in *Titus Andronicus*

> when Lavinia, by writing her attackers' name ... gains power over them. But to do so she puts Marcus's staff into her mouth creating a displaced image of the rape itself. She thus describes the rape at the cost of symbolically re-enacting it. The moment recalls one of the play's most disturbing images at the end of 3.1. Titus places his severed hand in Lavinia's mouth ... [Titus'] invasiveness is externalized in an image that, like the sight of Marcus's staff in her mouth, reenacts the original atrocity. (246)[33]

Some attempt to circumvent dealing with these horrors by suggesting Shakespeare didn't write these particular passages in *Titus Andronicus*, or that they are merely the excesses of an exuberant young poet's exaltation in his prodigious poetic skill. But, what if this image — of Lavinia with a staff in her mouth — lies at the very centre of Shakespeare's sensibility? Or, even more frightening, what if it lay at the centre of Shakespeare's lived experience? What if — like anyone who was traumatized — Shakespeare compulsively returned again and again to the scene of the traumatic incident, hoping that by confessing his emotional participation in an atrocity — and by describing that atrocity over and over — he might somehow come to understand it, *solve* it, and make it disappear?

The passage of time and the antique nature of Shakespeare's style has made it difficult to witness the urgency of Shakespeare's work. The distance we have from his work has also made it easy to classify it as comforting 'fine art' — and therefore, somehow, 'nice.' Undeniably, there were probably Nazi sadists who enjoyed reading a Shakespeare poem to take their mind off their crimes. And probably it would have been Shakespeare's sweetest, most mellifluous, most 'honey-tongued' passages that they would have turned to, again and again.

But, if we look at the entire Shakespearean canon and put it in the context of Shakespeare's many warnings — not just about the difficulty of expressing grief, but about the seductive illusions of art itself — we will find, at the centre of it all, a deeply intelligent person writing about a very personal pain. Yes, Shakespeare is aware of his own ability to distract us from the painful core that lies at the centre of his work, and yet, he is deeply conflicted about utilizing his poetic virtuosity in order to do so.

Something terrible happened to Shakespeare. Despite his affinity for comedy, despite his skepticism, his paradoxes, and his genre mixing, he was not simply a disinterested, bemused commentator. And yet scholars never tire of reminding us over and over that Shakespeare's primary virtue — and what separates him (strangely enough) from other writers — is that he *does not write about himself*. They *insist* that his work is *not* confessional, that it is *not* related to personal psychology or pathology. But, perhaps, we are afraid to ponder Shakespeare's personal life because we are afraid of what we might find there. By doing this, we deny Shakespeare the profundity of experience that most certainly accompanied the depth of his most trenchant observations.

Critics consistently avoid speculating on Shakespeare's life, even when the work demands it. Take this observation on *Hamlet* by T.S. Eliot:

> Why he attempted it at all is an insoluble puzzle; under compulsion of what experience he attempted to express the inexpressibly horrible, we cannot ever know. We need a great many facts

> in his biography ... We should have, finally, to know something which is by hypothesis unknowable, for we assume it to be an experience which, in the manner indicated, exceeded the facts. We should have to understand things which Shakespeare did not understand himself. (102)[34]

But that is precisely what artists do: try and understand what cannot be understood in a rational way. Shakespeare was not a philosopher or an ideologue — he turned to poetry —yes — *a*s a kind of therapy. Because — like T.S. Eliot — we are afraid of Shakespeare's work (and of the man behind it) so we have appropriated it in defence of the indefensible notion that the most profound artists must not, under any circumstance, transform their personal lives into poetry. In fact, we believe that the universality of great work demands that the work come from another place than the artist's suffering.

The opposite is true: every word Shakespeare wrote contained a deeply personal confession. In Sonnet 76, Shakespeare writes, "Why write I still all one, ever the same, / And keep invention in a noted weed, / That every word doth almost tell my name, / Showing their birth, and where they did proceed?" (90). [35] In *Shakespeare's Fingerprints*, Michael Brame suggests that with the phrase 'every word doth almost tell my name,' Edward de Vere is revealing, through wordplay — through a pun — that he is the real Shakespeare. For what de Vere is actually saying is 'a *vere-word* doth almost tell my name.' But what if de Vere is saying even more than that? What if he is saying, '*You will find me in my work*'?

In his personal life, the Earl of Oxford experienced *not only* great trauma, but, yes, also, a *kind of rape*. His life itself might have been a kind of 'atrocity.' And he was forever barred from ever telling his strange, complex, tragic story. De Vere was an aristocrat— he began life as one of the richest nobles in England — but he may well also have been one of the very few members of a very elite 'persecuted minority' who have rarely been able, under any circumstances, to reveal their truth.

What is commonly known as the 'Prince Tudor Theory' was introduced by Percy Allen in 1932, and later taken up by Charles and Dorothy Ogburn in their biography of the Earl of Oxford (*The Star of England*, 1952). The essence of the Prince Tudor Theory is that Queen Elizabeth and Edward de Vere were lovers. When Elizabeth was approximately forty — and de Vere was approximately twenty-three — they conceived a child: Henry Wriothesley, the Earl of Southampton. The sonnets were written to, and about, Henry Wriothesley. That is why the first seventeen sonnets urge the young man to marry. Wriothesley was, after all, betrothed to Edward de Vere's daughter, Elizabeth — and if they were to marry, then their children — like Wriothesley himself — would have been heirs to the throne. This historical aspect of the Prince Tudor Theory — the Tudor dynasty, the Essex Rebellion, Henry Wriothesley's imprisonment and his mysterious release — are all recounted in *Shakespeare's Sonnets*, and explained in detail in Hank Whittemore's *The Monument*.

A second, even more controversial Prince Tudor Theory (offered by Paul Streitz in *Oxford: Son of Elizabeth,* 2001) — 'Prince Tudor II' — states that Edward de Vere identified as King Edward the VII — and that his signature was in the shape of a crown until 1603, when James became king. Edward de Vere spent most of his life believing he had a claim to the throne because —according to Prince Tudor II — he was not *only* Queen Elizabeth's lover, but *her son*.

Is all this too much? Are we actually to believe that Queen Elizabeth gave birth out of wedlock to two sons — one with whom she had an affair— producing a baby who was his own father's brother? Some proponents of the 'Prince Tudor Theory' even believe that in *The Sonnets*, de Vere was expressing a sexual attraction to Henry Wriostheley. What's going on here? Was the reign of Queen Elizabeth I a hotbed of incest? Were the Tudors something akin to the Borgias? Many of those who believe de Vere was Shakespeare have no time for the Prince Tudor Theory— as the idea seems amoral, objectionable, and just too unlikely to even consider.

Or is it?

The concept of incest was far from alien to Elizabeth I. When Elizabeth was eleven, she translated Marguerite, Queen of Navarre's, French poem *The Glass of the Sinful Soul.* It's difficult to find information about this book. What is usually said is that the book has a very pretty cover. Indeed it does, apparently painstakingly embroidered by young Elizabeth herself. But the French original of *The Glass of the Sinful Soul* was written by a young French princess (Marguerite de Navarre) whose brother was the king of France. Her situation was very similar to Elizabeth's (as Elizabeth was also the sister of a future king — Edward VI). Elizabeth's translation speaks not only to her monumental learning (she knew six languages by the age of eleven), but also her wide-ranging philosophical and religious meditations.

In the original poem, Marguerite de Navarre attempts to explain her relationship with her brother by comparing it to a relationship with Christ. In a review of Mark Shell's *Elisabeth's Glass,* Sara Jayne Steen recounts Shell's comments about Elizabeth's translation, saying it interprets the text

> in light of 'universal siblinghood,' his [Shell's) term for the doctrine in which all humans are brothers and sisters in Christ — and therefore, he maintains, all sexual intercourse incestuous — Shell proposes that the sinful soul, bound by what

> Elizabeth translates as "concupiscence," is enslaved by desire for incest. *The Glass of the Sinful Soul* in that context reveals physical incest transcended by a spiritual incest in which God is father, brother, son, and husband.[36]

Why would Elizabeth translate such a poem into English at the age of eleven? Perhaps the notion that 'all sex is incest' would have appealed to her because it would have let her mother (Ann Boleyn) off the hook — as well as herself. After all, Henry VIII's excuse for divorcing Ann Boleyn was that she had committed incest with her brother; and, as a result, Elizabeth was deemed a bastard child.

It's quite natural that historians might gloss over this juicy tidbit of literary history as it's upsetting to think about a young girl at the tender age of eleven entertaining such radical sexual ideas. But in early modern times, the notion that kings and queens were of royal blood (a 'blood' that is often referred to in Shakespeare's plays), and that this blood was in some way blessed — that it was God's blood — was not just a fancy. Because royals were related to God, it was thought that by having sex with each other, they were keeping their precious blood 'in the family.' All of this leads one to believe that the possibility of Elizabeth entertaining the idea of having sex with her own son might not have been as unlikely as it might seem to us today.

We have no proof that Elizabeth had children. But it is quite possible the mantle of 'virgin queen' was one that she wore out of necessity, as she seemed to have had a horror of marriage. Elisabeth was fourteen when de Vere was born, and, at the time, she was likely having an affair with the brother of Henry VIII's wife: Thomas Seymour. At one point Seymour proposed marriage to her. At various times in Elizabeth's life, there was gossip about the queen's 'licentiousness.' We don't know for sure what Elisabeth was up to later, in 1572-3. There are conflicting reports, some of which suggest a possible confinement from pregnancy, while various others do not. But we do know for certain that, when he was approximately twenty-three, the young Edward de Vere had replaced Robert Dudley in the queen's affections. As Hank Whittemore notes, Gilbert Talbot would write to his father the Earl of Shrewsbury from Court on May 11, 1573: "My Lord of Oxford is lately grown into great credit, for the Queen's Majesty delighteth more in his personage and his dancing and valiantness than any other ... If it were not for his fickle head, he would pass any of them shortly."[37] We also know that in 1571 — oddly and coincidentally — the Treason Act was ruled to negate 'the law of primogeniture,' which means that it was suddenly legal for any illegitimate child of Elizabeth to claim the throne. [38]

That the young Edward de Vere may have been the victim of the advances of an older woman who was his mother — who also happened to be the Queen of England — is a story that de Vere would have wanted desperately to tell, not only because he believed he was the rightful heir to the throne, but because it was for him, a tortured truth that, if left unspoken, might burn a hole in his heart. This explains his choice of subject matter in his most inscrutable works: *Venus and Adonis*, *The Rape of Lucrece*, and *Titus Andronicus*, and might shed some light on Hamlet's obsession with his mother, and Shakespeare's obsession with the 'dark lady' - the personification of sex and sexuality — in *The Sonnets.*

It would also explain Shakespeare's attraction to the tale of Actaeon, and the sobbing deer. This story is key to Shakespeare's personal psychology. Shakespeare refers to it constantly, not only by making direct reference to the story, but in his persistent — sometimes glancing — references to 'horns' and 'cuckolding.'

It's no surprise that the tale of Actaeon, as told by Ovid, is a story about sex. A young hunter is tempted when he accidentally catches sight of the goddess Artemis (read: Roman goddess Diana) bathing naked. To punish him, Artemis turns Actaeon into a stag. She also sets his own hounds on him. *He is then ripped apart by his own dogs*. (This detail is important — as it explains why this myth is central to Shakespeare's life.) Keep in mind that the goddess Diana was often associated with Elizabeth, as John. N. King observes: "Modern scholarship associates the moon goddess Diana (or Cynthia) with the praise of Elizabeth's chastity...the "moon cult" of Elizabeth as a perpetually virgin goddess emerged and took root after the failure of her last effort at marriage" (916).[38]

Besides the reference to the sobbing deer in *As You Like It*, there are at least four other direct references to Actaeon in Shakespeare's work, including *Titus Andronicus, Twelfth Night, Cymbeline*, and *The Merry Wives of Windsor.* Tamora in *Titus Andronicus* wishes she was Diana, so Bassanius' "temples should be planted presently / With horns, as was Acteon's ..." (2.3.61-62).[39] When Orsino in *Twelfth Night* speaks of love, he says,

> Oh, when mine eyes did see Olivia first,
> Methought she purged the air of pestilence.
> That instant was I turned into a hart,
> And my desires, like fell and cruel hounds,
> E'er since pursue me. (1.1. 20-24)[40]

In *Cymbeline*, Iachomo sneaks into Imogen's bedroom and — like the voyeur Actaeon — observes her naked breasts. In the *Merry Wives of Windsor*, it is the ever 'horny' John Falstaff who is symbolically turned into a stag, ridiculed, and adorned with horns.

In addition to these instances where a reference to Actaeon, the stag, means, essentially, 'horny,' there are many instances where the mere mention of 'horns' is a surefire laugh trigger, a seemingly perfect joke. Shakespeare returns to it again and again. Today, when we read this antique jest, it's not clear why it's funny. But, to an early modern audience, 'horns' meant cuckolding. However, isn't a cuckolded man the very opposite of a horny man — the cuckold is, after all, a fool for not being successful in controlling his wife's libido? Do Acteon's horns mean a horny man or a cuckold?

It turns out that for Shakespeare and his audience it meant both. In early modern times, men who lusted after women were not admired in the same way they are today. Promiscuous heterosexual males are still (despite the protestations of #METOO activists) admired by other straight men. A 'playboy' or womanizer or ladykiller, is viewed as a 'real' man by other men in the privacy of the locker room. Women may criticize such creatures, but it's not a very well kept secret that lots of men harbour fantasies of having lots of different female partners to play with. In the early modern period, men had the same urges, but those urges were viewed quite differently by other men. A 'ladies man' or 'wolf' or 'rotter' was not so much disapproved of as thought to be *not* a 'real man.' Many viewed men who chased after women not only to be fools but to be *less than men*; in fact, they were accused of effeminacy in the same way gay men are today. They were, in effect, wasting their masculinity by chasing after women, and thus becoming more like women themselves. (This is Antony's problem in *Antony and Cleopatra.*)

Agnès Lafont suggests that in *Merry Wives of Windsor*, Actaeon's horns, "a symbol of his voyeurism and his immoderate desires, become the horn of the assumed cuckold ... more crudely, the allusion to Actaeon's horns may also provide a useful subtext to mention sexual intercourse."[41] Actaeon, therefore, generally means 'sex,' is an eloquent symbol of the power of sex, and, as such, represents a paradox. Lafont goes on to list the many meanings of Shakespeare's Actaeon:

> Actaeon as a voyeur, as a guilty intruder (or as an unlucky young man); Actaeon as a hunted hunter, Actaeon as a political intruder, Actaeon as a dismembered man, Actaeon as a cuckold. Among the various segments of the myth that are evoked by Shakespeare, it seems that a unifying and convincing theme is that of the gaze and the dangers it carries both for the person that is spied upon and for the viewer.[42]

The lustful man is, in Shakespeare's terms, pursued by his own hounds. The cuckolded man, and paradoxically, his opposite — the man who cuckolds him — are both victims of lust, and therefore both are Actaeon, and both must wear 'the horns.' If Shakespeare had sex with his own mother, he may have blamed himself; he may have blamed his own desire; he may have decided that sex was "th'expense of spirit in a waste of shame" (639),[43] and that even his own 'heart' was a 'hart' that would be pursued and eventually ripped apart by the 'dogs' of his *own* desire.

The purpose here is not to convince you that the Earl of Oxford was Shakespeare, or that Queen Elizabeth was his mother and his lover. We need not go to historical records for proof; we need only read the work. Being seduced by your mother as a young man would certainly be traumatic, and would perhaps be the closest a male might come to the experience of being raped.

Or perhaps, Shakespeare was not Edward de Vere at all. Perhaps he was not 'raped' by Elizabeth. But if it was not that *particular* atrocity that tortured him, then it most certainly was something else. For *there was a horror*. And it was one of which Shakespeare was unable to speak without fear of enormous reprisal and significant humiliation. If what survivors of the Holocaust say is true (and if it is true what Shakespeare himself wrote), then those who experience the deepest horrors not only inevitably struggle with how they might be expressed, but also with the fundamental ethics of speaking those truths at all. Yet, they feel inexorably compelled to do so. And if — as Sontag proposes — this compulsory silencing can create new sensibilities, and sometimes be the origin of great art, then it seems to me almost certainly, that at the very least, *something terrible happened to Shakespeare*. And he could not ever, *ever* tell anyone about it.

But in his own way, he did.

This is not to say that we must 'interpret' Shakespeare's work or attempt to translate it and find its true 'message.' Nor does it mean that his work is about any psychoanalysis that we might impose on him. It does not mean that I or anyone else should require that you accept their explanation of what Shakespeare's particular personal torture was. That is the last thing he would want. But that he would have wanted his work to stand — as Hank Whittemore says — as a kind of 'monument' to a life that was as chaotic and beautiful as so many of our lives — simply means this: Shakespeare recognized that it was not the 'message' that would remain after his death. His poems are not, after all, 'virtuous' works. They are, simply, beautiful ones.

Endnotes

1 Shakespeare, William. T*he Taming of the Shrew*. Arden Shakespeare, 2010.

2 Shakespeare, William. T*he Taming of the Shrew*.

[3] Burns, Timothy W. "Philosophy and Poetry: A New Look At An Old Quarrel." *American Political Science Review* Vol. 109, No. 2, 2015.

[4] Burns, Timothy W. "Philosophy and Poetry: A New Look At An Old Quarrel."

[5] Burns, Timothy W. "Philosophy and Poetry: A New Look At An Old Quarrel."

[6] Shakespeare, William. Much Ado About Nothing. Oxford University Press, 1993.

[7] Shakespeare, William. Romeo and Juliet. (New Folger's ed.), Washington Square Press/Pocket Books, 2004

[8] Shakespeare, William. *Hamlet*. (New Folger's ed.), Washington Square Press/Pocket Books, 2012.

[9] Gray, Patrick. "Shakespeare vs. Seneca: competing visions of human dignity" *Brill's Companion to the Reception of Senecan Tragedy.* (Eric Dodson Robinson, ed.) Vol 5. Leiden, 2016.

[10] Gray, Patrick. "Shakespeare vs. Seneca: competing visions of human dignity"

[11] Shakespeare, William. *Titus Andronicus.* (New Folger's ed.), Washington Square Press/Pocket Books, 2005.

[12] McGilchrist, Iain. *The Master and His Emissary*. Yale University Press, 2009.

[13] Shakespeare, William. *The Merchant of Venice.* Signet, 1987.

[14] McGilchrist, Iain. *The Master and His Emissary*. Yale University Press, 2009.

[15] Shakespeare, William. *As You Like It.* (New Folger's ed.), Washington Square Press/Pocket Books, 1997.

[16] Shakespeare, William. *As You Like It.*

[17] Shakespeare, William. "Lucrece." *The Complete Sonnets and Poems*. Oxford University Press, 2002.

[18] Shakespeare, William. *As You Like It.*

[19] Willis, Deborah. "'The Gnawing Vulture': Revenge, Trauma Theory, and 'Titus Andronicus'" *Shakespeare Quarterly* Vol. 53, No. 1, Oxford University Press.

[20] Willis, Deborah. "'The Gnawing Vulture': Revenge, Trauma Theory, and 'Titus Andronicus'" *Shakespeare Quarterly* Vol. 53, No. 1, Oxford University Press.

[21] Fox, Cora. *Ovid and the Politics of Emotion in Elizabethan England.* Palgrave and MacMillan, 2009.

[22] Fox, Cora. *Ovid and the Politics of Emotion in Elizabethan England.* Palgrave and MacMillan, 2009.

[23] Shakespeare, William. *Richard II.* (New Folger's ed.). Washington Square Press/Pocket Books, 2010.

[24] Shakespeare, William. *Richard II.*

[25] Shakespeare, William. *Richard II.*

[26] Shakespeare, William. *Hamlet*. (New Folger's ed.), Washington Square Press/Pocket Books, 2012.

[27] Shakespeare William. *Titus Andronicus*. (New Folger's ed.).,Washington Square Press/Pocket Books, 2010.

[28] Adorno, Theodor W. "Cultural Criticism and Society." *Prisms.* MIT Press, 1983.

[29] "Jean François Lyotard." *Stanford Encyclopedia of Philosophy.* (https://plato.stanford.edu/entries/lyotard/.

[30] "Jean François Lyotard." *Stanford Encyclopedia of Philosophy.*

[31] Sontag, Susan. *Against Interpretation*. Dell, 1966.

[32] Shakespeare, William. *Macbeth*. (New Folger's ed.), Washington Square Press/Pocket Books, 2013.

[33] Shakespeare William. *Titus Andronicus*. (New Folger's ed.), Washington Square Press/Pocket Books, 2010.

[34] Eliot, T.S. *The Sacred Wood*. Methuen & Company Ltd., 1950.

[35] Shakespeare, William. *Sonnets*. Oxford University Press, 2003.

[36] Steen, Jayne. "Review of Elizabeth's Glass." *Renaissance Quarterly.* Vol. 48, Issue 4 *The Renaissance Society of America.* Cambridge University Press, 1995.

[37] Whittemore, Hank. https://hankwhittemore.com/2013/04/06/christopher-hatton-and-malvolio-part-two-of-reason-68-why-the-earl-of-oxford-was-shakespeare/

[38] King, John N. "Queen Elizabeth I: Representations of the Virgin Queen." Source: *Renaissance Quarterly.* Vol. 43, No. 1. Cambridge University Press, 1990.

[39] Shakespeare, William. *Titus Andronicus*. (New Folger's ed.), Washington Square Press/Pocket Books,2010.

[40] Shakespeare, William. *Twelfth Night*.(New Folger's ed.), Washington Square Press/Pocket Books, 2009.

[41] Lafont, Agnès. "Shakespeare's Myths." *A Dictionary of Shakespeare's Classical Mythology.* http://www.shakmyth.org/myth/4/actaeon/analysis

[42] Lafont, Agnès . "Shakespeare's Myths." *A Dictionary of Shakespeare's Classical Mythology.*

[43] Shakespeare, William. "Sonnet 129." *Complete Sonnets and Poems*. Oxford University Press, 2002.

Epilogue: Lies

Art is a lie. And Shakespeare was the greatest liar of all. That the premiere poet in English was not particularly interested in reason, logic, or in moralizing, does not mean he thought we have no need for these things, but that he cared about an older aesthetic tradition. At no time in history have we ever so badly needed to understand the nature of lying. For, suddenly, truth is nowhere to be found. Donald Trump has entranced the multitudes with a simple, yet genuinely beautiful, alliterative lie. His January 6th motto: 'Stop the Steal,' is a short and brutally bewitching poem; it may initiate a second American civil war.

The truth is that we need lies. And we *will* have them one way or the other. Have you ever tried to press out a bubble on your iPhone screen protector — only to have it pop up somewhere else? Just when we think we are rid of lies, they appear again. Life is unfathomable and unreasonable, and living by reason alone is not *really living*. When denied the irrational, and ordered not to be 'intuitive,' we inevitably find a beautiful lie and cling to it for dear life. Simply put, we are not *merely* rational beings. There are more things in heaven and earth than are dreamt of in post-enlightenment philosophy. What separates human beings from animals is not just an exquisite capacity for reason, but also a predominating passion for lying.

According to McGilchrist, Shakespeare's work personifies an expansive right brain view with a "complete disregard for theory and for category, a celebration of multiplicity and the richness of human variety, rather than the rehearsal of common laws" (304).[1] This obsession brings us characters "such as Falstaff, that are incomprehensible in terms of the element into which they could be analyzed, but form Gestalt-like, new, coherent, living wholes" (304).[2] This was Shakespeare's genius: that the richness of it is only comprehensible to us because we must perceive it as a complete, paradoxical, complex entity, one that cannot be broken into parts. McGilchrist says we enjoy music — an activity unique to the right brain — in much the same manner we enjoy Shakespeare's work: "Its indivisible nature, the necessity of experiencing the whole at any one time ... makes it the natural language of the right hemisphere" (73).[3]

Trying to pick apart Shakespeare's work in search of a moral lesson is not only in vain, but it goes against the very essence of his anti-dialectical project. In *Against Interpretation* (1966), Sontag writes eloquently against parsing a work of art into its component parts in search of meaning, The endless, fruitless interpretation of Shakespeare's work has paralyzed Shakespeare studies. Academics battle endlessly over what Shakespeare *really means* — when he meant merely everything and merely nothing at all. For Sontag,

> Interpretation is the revenge of the intellect upon art. Even more, it is the revenge of the intellect upon the world, to interpret is to impoverish, to deplete the world — in order to set up a shadow of 'meanings.' It is to turn *the* world into *this* world ... The world, our world, is impoverished enough. (98-99)[4]

Sontag and Barthes have called for an erotics of art. They demand we think in the manner of medieval grammarians who believed the world was a book — one we must learn to read, once again, like Adam and Eve. This can only be achieved through poetry.

The recent intrusion of the woke left into aesthetics is consistent with a skewed and dangerous left brain dominance, and it threatens to destroy art. The woke folks don't like being accused of being a religious cult. No, like the leaders of the French Revolution, they imagine themselves as applying logic to the dangerous irrationality of art: and, indeed, the plot and characters of every work must be broken down into their component parts and analyzed for meaning. Martha Schabas' article in the November 28, 2017 *Globe and Mail* is typical of the new impatience with 'objectionable ideas' that crowds these old illusions; she demands that ballets provide new, less sexist content, complaining of "John Neumeier's *A Streetcar Named Desire* [which] featured the long, explicit rape of Blanche, in which Stanley brutalized her in 10-odd minutes of violent choreography. In the company's version of Swan Lake, choreographed by James Kudelka, the first act ends with the gang rape of a character called 'the wench.'"[5]

Canadian theatre is presently overrun by 'social justice warriors' — a shadowy but ever present thought police that monitors our work. The few theatre productions that we were able to see outdoors or online during COVID were relentlessly preachy.

Don't get me wrong. In fact, I generally agree with many of the ideas promoted by social justice warriors, and, in this sense at least, I am on their side. However, they are bringing tools of analysis that belong in a science lab or a university lecture hall into a theatre. Art cannot — should not — be analyzed in this way. For if the job of the artist is only to decorate ideas prettily in order to entice us into believing them, then art is merely education — or worse yet, propaganda.

I am gay. I write novels, plays, and poems with gay subject matter. But I am proud that I have *never* succeeded at educating people about how wonderful homosexuality is. After my first Toronto hit play *The Dressing Gown*, in 1985 I was approached by the lead actress in my production — earnestly — with this question: 'Why do you hate gay men so much?" In my own small way, I am the gay equivalent of Mordecai Richler, detested by his own Jewish community in Montreal for being antisemitic. Richler wrote about 'real' Jewish people in his novel *The Apprenticeship of Duddy Kravitz*. Richler's Jews — like Shakespeare's Kings and Queens — were not models of virtue, but all too flawed and human. I write about flawed gay men. For instance, the principal characters in my play *Drag Queens in Outer Space* are not squeaky clean victims preaching about their oppression (like the pitiful gals you see on RuPaul's *Drag Race*). My drag queens are not ideologues; by their own admission, they "live by the skin of their spike heels" (408).[6]

I have paid the price for writing from my imagination rather than from a need to educate and spread 'truth.' As I mentioned in the introduction, the re-mount of my play *Drag Queens in Outer Space* was cancelled in 2018 due to objections from the woke left over my blog "I'm Afraid of Woke People." At approximately the same time, I lost my publisher of twenty years: ECW Press. When I asked ECW why they had stopped publishing my novels, they told me that decisions were now being made by committee. I have no doubt that the committee had extended discussions about me, and weighed the pros and cons of my work, analyzed it, and interpreted it — ideologically — and that my art was found wanting — but only after it was reduced to the sum of whatever scandalous notions could be yanked out and summarily denounced as offensive. I don't ask for your pity. I am one of many of the victims of the new puritan woke left. Anne Applebaum observes,

> Right here in America, right now, it is possible to meet people who have lost everything — jobs, money, friends, colleagues — after violating no laws, and sometimes no workplace rules either. Instead, they have broken (or are accused of having broken) social codes having to do with race, sex, personal behaviour, or even acceptable humour, which may not have existed five years ago or maybe five months ago. Some have made egregious errors of judgment. Some have done nothing at all. It is not always easy to tell.[7]

I don't speak about this alarming trend for myself — or on behalf of others who have been 'cancelled' (in far more serious ways) — but in the name of art.

Shakespeare knew that art was a lie. He seemed worried we might forget, as he defined it that way over and over again. In *Cymbeline*, Posthumous is confused by his own tumultuous life until it is revealed to him in a dream that his family (who are now dead), and the god Jupiter, support him. When he wakes up from the dream, he is holding a book: "What fairies haunt this ground? A book?" (5.4. 137).[8] The text is a mysterious parable which he doesn't even try to explain:

> 'Tis still a dream, or else such stuff as madmen
> Tongue, and brain not, either both, or nothing,
> Or senseless speaking, or a speaking such
> As sense cannot untie. Be what it is,
> The action of my life is like it, which I'll keep
> If but for sympathy. (5.4.148-153)[9]

A poem, like life, is a dream, and it cannot be logically explicated in words. However, when we read a poem or a novel, or see a play, a dance, or a film, or listen to a symphony, the experience seems somehow, in some odd way, to reflect our own life. The comfort this brings is eternal, but not in any way definable.

I will compare myself to Shakespeare in this way. I have no doubt that — whatever the scandalous nature of his real life — it was the scandalous nature of *his work* that caused it to be largely ignored until Garrick's Shakespeare Jubilee of 1769. The many contradictory ideologies offered by his work, the characters that it was impossible to classify as heroes or villains — and perhaps the unimaginable horror of the pain that was evidently its source — *this* is what was responsible for the strange appearance of the perplexing 'First Folio' of 1623, edited by Ben Jonson. That infamous collection is accompanied by an inept drawing of a man who looks more like a joker in a pack of cards than a poet — and to top it all off, Jonson's mysterious introduction is brimful of riddling innuendo.

I have no doubt that Shakespeare — who I believe, in real life, was Edward de Vere — lied about his identity because of some deeply scandalous and traumatic secret in his personal life. But the lie of art, that Shakespeare effectively invented, is the real gift of his work. It is from Shakespeare that we can learn deeply and beautifully about both the danger and romance of deception. And, if God forbid, we someday forget how important deception is, we may be buried alive by the avalanche of untruths that descend upon us when the lie of art is gone.

Endnotes

1 McGilchrist, lain. *The Master and His Emissary*. Yale University Press, 2009.

2 McGilchrist, lain.

3 McGilchrist, lain.

4 Sontag, Susan. *Against Interpretation.* Dell, 1966.

5 Schabas, Martha. "How we make excuses for violence against women onstage" *The Globe and Mail*. https://www.theglobeandmail.com/arts/theatre-and-performance/how-we-make-excuses-for-violence-against-women-on-stage/article37114673/ 2017.

6 Gilbert, Sky. "Drag Queens on Trial." *Modern Canadian Plays.* Jerry Wasserman, ed. Talonbooks 2000.

7 Applebaum, Anne. "Mob Justice is threatening Democratic Discourse." *The Atlantic.* https://www.theatlantic.com/magazine/archive/2021/10/new-puritans-mob-justice-canceled/619818/, 2021.

8 Shakespeare, William. *Cymbeline*. (New Folger's ed.), Washington Square Press/Pocket Books, 2003.

9 Shakespeare, William. *Cymbeline*. (New Folger's ed.), Washington Square Press/Pocket Books, 2003.

Acknowledgements

Special thanks to Margo Anderson, Ken Anstruther, Sally Clark, Michele Muzzi, Hank Whittemore, and Ian Jarvis for their astute suggestions.

About the Author

Sky Gilbert is a poet, novelist, playwright, filmmaker, theatre director, and drag queen extraordinaire. He was co-founder and artistic director of Toronto's Buddies in Bad Times Theatre — one of the world's largest gay and lesbian theatres — from 1979 to 1997. He has had more than 40 plays produced, and written 9 critically acclaimed novels and three award winning poetry collections. He has received three Dora Mavor Moore Awards as well as the Pauline McGibbon Award, The Silver Ticket Award, the ReLit Award for his novel *An English Gentleman a*nd most recently The Violet Prize at Blue Metropolis literary Festival for his body of work. There is a street in Toronto named after him: 'Sky Gilbert Lane.' He is presently working on his 10th full length novel, *The Blue House*, to be published by Cormorant, also in 2024, as well as a third book about Shakespeare, tentatively titled 'Shakespeare's Effeminacy'. Dr. Gilbert is a Professor Emeritus at the University of Guelph (where he taught theatre and creative writing from 1998-2022).

Printed by Imprimerie Gauvin
Gatineau, Québec